Ellina Abdul Majid is the author of two novels, *Perhaps in Paradise* (longlisted for the International IMPAC Dublin Literary Award 1999) and *Khairunnisa: A Good Woman*; and a children's book, *Iguanas In Our Garden*.

Ellina was educated in Malaysia and the UK. After receiving her primary and early secondary school education at Convent Bukit Nanas Kuala Lumpur, she was packed off to a boarding school in England, where to her astonishment, Art, Literature and Music were subjects held in the same high regard as Maths and Physics. She holds a BA Hons in Law & Anthropology from SOAS, University of London and a Diploma in Speech & Drama from LAMDA (London Academy of Music & Dramatic Art), UK.

She divides her time between her home in KL, her dusun in Gombak and her tiny flat in London's Royal Borough of Kensington & Chelsea. But she is happiest when trekking deep in the Malaysian jungle with her little bear, Buncit, for company.

FIXI NOVO MANIFESTO

1. WE BELIEVE THAT OMPUTIH/GWAILOH-SPEAK
IS A MALAYSIAN LANGUAGE.

2. WE USE AMERICAN SPELLING. THIS IS BECAUSE
WE ARE MORE INFLUENCED BY HOLLYWOOD THAN
THE HOUSE OF WINDSOR.

3. WE PUBLISH STORIES ABOUT THE URBAN REALITY OF
MALAYSIA. IF YOU WANT TO SHARE YOUR GRANDMOTHER'S
WORLD WAR 2 STORIES, SEND 'EM ELSEWHERE AND YOU
MIGHT EVEN WIN THE BOOKER PRIZE.

4. WE SPECIALIZE IN PULP FICTION, BECAUSE CRIME,
HORROR, SCI-FI AND SO ON TURN US ON.

5. WE WILL NOT USE ITALICS FOR NON-AMERICAN/
NON-ENGLISH TERMS. THIS IS BECAUSE THOSE WORDS ARE
NOT FOREIGN TO A MALAYSIAN AUDIENCE. SO WE WILL NOT
HAVE "THEY HAD *NASI LEMAK* AND WENT BACK TO *KONGKEK*"
BUT RATHER "THEY HAD NASI LEMAK AND WENT BACK TO
KONGKEK". NASI LEMAK AND KONGKEK ARE SOME OF THE
PLEASURES OF MALAYSIAN LIFE THAT SHOULD BE CELEBRATED
WITHOUT APOLOGY; ITALICS ARE A FORM OF APOLOGY.

6. WE PUBLISH NOVELS AND SHORT-STORY ANTHOLOGIES.
WE DON'T PUBLISH POETRY; WE LIKE MAKING MONEY.

7. THE EXISTING MALAYSIAN BOOKS THAT COME CLOSEST
TO WHAT WE WANNA DO: *DEVIL'S PLACE* BY BRIAN GOMEZ;
AND THE INSPECTOR MISLAN CRIME NOVELS BY
ROZLAN MOHD NOOR. LOOK FOR THEM!

8. WE PUBLISH BOOKS WITH THE SAME PRINT RUN
AND THE SAME PRICE AS THOSE OF OUR PARENT COMPANY,
BUKU FIXI. SO A BOOK OF ABOUT 300 PAGES WILL SELL
AT RM20. THIS IS BECAUSE WE WANNA REACH OUT TO THE
YOUNG, THE SENGKEK AND THE KIAM SIAP.

CALL FOR ENTRIES.

INTERESTED? FOR NOVELS,
SEND YOUR SYNOPSIS AND FIRST 2 CHAPTERS.
FOR ANTHOLOGIES, SEND A SHORT STORY OF BETWEEN
2,000-5,000 WORDS ON THE THEME "KL NOIR."
SEND TO INFO@FIXI.COM.MY ANYTIME.

CRÈME DE LA CRIME: PI ROMY & THE HAVE-HAVES

×

ELLINA ABDUL MAJID

ILLUSTRATIONS BY

RAYYAN IRFAN CHAI

NOVO

Published by
Fixi Novo *which is an imprint of:*
Buku Fixi Sdn Bhd (1174441-X)
B-8-2A Opal Damansara, Jalan PJU 3/27
47810 Petaling Jaya, Malaysia
info@fixi.com.my
http://fixi.com.my

This is a work of fiction. All the perpetrators depicted in each story are, fortuitously, merely figments of the author's fertile imagination.

The lyrics quoted in *PI Romy Sees The Big Picture* are from the songs 'If The World Was Ending' (written & performed by JP Saxe, feat Julia Michaels), '50 Ways To Leave Your Lover' (written & performed by Paul Simon), 'Sweet Dreams' (written by Annie Lennox & Dave Stewart, performed by The Eurhythmics) and 'Asyik' (written by Dedi Abdul Kadir Nugraha & performed by Amelina).

Extracts from the poem 'Will There Really be a Morning' by Emily Dickinson and 'He Wishes for the Cloths of Heaven' by W. B. Yeats are quoted in the story *PI Romy Listens With His Eyes*.

Crème De La Crime:
PI Romy & The Have-haves
© Ellina Abdul Majid

First Print: December 2021

Cover design by Iskander Azizuddin, front cover photo reproduced with kind permission of Biswajit Guha.
Layout: Teck Hee
Consultants: Amir Muhammad & Ted Mahsun

ISBN 978-967-2328-76-6
Catalogue-in-Publication Data available from the National Library of Malaysia.

Printed by:
Vinlin Press Sdn Bhd
2 Jalan Meranti Permai 1, Meranti Permai Industrial Park
Batu 15, Jalan Puchong, 47100 Puchong, Malaysia

A Special Note To The Reader

Avid readers often like to create pictures in their minds' eye as part of their enjoyment of a story. The illustrations which accompany each PI Romy story were skillfully imagined and drawn by 9 year-old Rayyan Irfan Chai, whose grandmother Sharifah Rokaiyah attended the same bourgie boarding school in the UK as Ellina.

A prolific artist since the age of 4, Rayyan's dedication and zeal have enabled him to sell his merchandise side by side with other professional adult artists at the Artists' Corner, Amcorp Mall. When asked what he aspires to achieve in the not-too-distant future, Rayyan's exuberant reply is that he has a series of comics in the making, which he hopes will appeal to comic fans everywhere!

$$\times$$

Ellina's current foray into writing crime stories arose purely by accident, when one of her sons casually suggested she enter the KL Noir 2021 short story competition. The prize was RM200 for each story selected, to be published in the anthology *KL Noir: Magic*.

Alas, her story never made the selection but she had enjoyed writing it so much, she went on to write eight more. All of them, as with the first, were written entirely on her iPhone 8 over several months, whenever she had a spare moment.

Ellina credits her husband Azizuddin and their children for her perseverance, in a maxim their family likes to go by: 'For when the one great scorer comes, to write against your name, he writes not that you won or lost, *but how you played the game*.'

The name of her detective, PI Romy, came about when she decided to seek inspiration on a staycay at a modest hotel in KL's quintessentially noir part of town.

Azizuddin thoughtfully ordered her a Grab ride so she would be spared parking issues. "It's a Perodua Bezza and the driver's name is Romy Irwan Shah." Serendipity.

✕

The front cover design was inspired by a chance WhatsApp convo between Ellina and her cousin Biswajit, who sent her a photo of himself with a cat, which had suddenly and inexplicably turned up at his home in Indonesia, where he currently works. Another purrfect serendipity moment.

Contents

✕

'Musuh melanggar ku gempur
Sungguh rela ku gugur kerana
Kau tanah pusaka...
Negaraku yang berdaulat dan merdeka'

- lagu patriotik 'Tanah Pusaka' karya Ahmad Merican,
lirik oleh Wan Ahmad Kamal & Dol Ramli

✕

To the memory of my father, Abdul Majid bin Ismail
(1921-2013), who always enjoyed a good story and
encouraged me to write my own.

1

✕

PI ROMY & THE DATIN IN DISTRESS

✕

It was 11.35 am.

PI Romy was having a crappy morning which looked set to extend to a crappy afternoon.

He realized it invariably panned out that way every time his first call of the day was from his ex-wife.

"Aiman needs a new laptop."

"Ya, I'll order one today."

"That's what you said last week, and please don't say, 'ya'. It's 'yes'."

For the umpteenth time, Romy wondered how he could ever have fallen in love with and married a teacher. An English language teacher.

WTF was he thinking?

Then he remembered. *Of course!* It was all his mother's fault, nagging him to get married. As though marriage was a panacea for everything that felt wrong in one's life.

On the bright side, his ex-wife had been the bitter pill but Aiman was the blessed cure.

"'Kay, kay. I'll order the laptop."

"I shall call you again tomorrow."

"Ya, uh yes, you do that. Darling."

His ex-wife hung up immediately.

Romy chuckled drily. That never failed to bait her.

The next blight on his day was his car battery dying on him, so it meant getting to his office via Grab, which he loathed. Every Grab driver he'd met thought being a Private Investigator was "Waah, glamour, 'bang."

In the end, he took to saying he sold insurance, which meant the journey could continue in blissful silence.

Of course, it had to be this same morning that his clerk messaged in sick, so he had to do all the menials.

Very dreary.

His office was merely a dingy space on the top floor of a shophouse, overlooking what politically incorrect locals cynically referred to as Bangla Square, with its bizarre installation of metal swings and a bunch of burst pipes, disguised as a fountain.

Then there was the clock tower. Another bone of contention which contributed to strained relations with his then wife and led to their breakup.

"It's Art Deco form at its most aesthetic, Romy. Isn't that sunburst motif exquisite?"

"Huh, what? The whole thing just looks like a dick to me. A short one, at that."

"Philistine."

Romy hated it when she suddenly changed the subject. "Of course I support Palestine. It's my duty as a Muslim."

As usual, he'd forgotten his pass key. Which meant looking for the Punjabi jaga at one of the mamaks in the vicinity, who always seemed to know when Romy was behind in the rental. Which then, also meant every mamak stall within a radius of 1 km would know too. *Urrgh.*

One thing after another, there was something wrong with the WiFi.

Damn.

Just when there were several reports and billing reminders to be sent out.

The daily reports to desperate Datins obsessed with notions of their straying husbands were the most tedious. Amazing though, how despite the pandemic and the havoc it caused on all aspects of life, it was invariably the lust thing that was on their minds.

But the money was good.

And Romy wasn't averse to buttering both sides of his bread. Why not, everyone had a right to cari makan.

"Datin hired me to spy on you."

"Hmm. How much for you to close one eye?"

"5k, Boss."

"Get lost."

"Alamak, sori Boss. My phone recorder was on, I didn't know."

"Here's 3k. Now, you better make sure you get lost."

"Don't be angry, Boss. I'm helping you."

Actually, Romy hated having to do that. But civilian life was tough to adapt to and living in KL wasn't cheap.

For the longest time, he'd actually harbored secret ambitions to be an actor.

Heck, with a name like Romy Irwan Shah, why ever not?

He had the height and build. But there were other boxes which had to be ticked, as far as casting agents and filmmakers were concerned.

So he'd applied to join the army instead. Which wasn't all bad. Sometimes it played out like an action movie, except that after the carnage and desolation, there was no reassuring shout of "Okay! Cut!" And also, ya, one just had to pray not to have to make it home draped under a flag.

Such was life.

Anyway, how many of the billions of people who walked the earth ever got to live their dream, despite all those MLM twats on social media swearing otherwise?

Meanwhile, there were more blights to blacken Romy's morning and mood.

Nothing wrong with the WiFi, he just hadn't paid the bill, that was all, so the WiFi had been disconnected, damnit.

His clerk had discreetly also left an opened letter from the bank.

It was the standard threat to repossess Romy's apartment for arrears in loan repayment.

This was definitely harassment, Romy fumed. Hadn't the government imposed a moratorium on loan repayment because of this Covid shit, which was killing everyone?

Whaat? He read the letter again. He was in arrears for so many months oredi?

Crap, he could feel an anime worry sweat coming on.

Best to take his mind off by checking the news instead. See if there were any updates on the murder of that big-shot Dato', who coincidentally had been one of his clients. But then, KL was quite small really.

Cocky bugger, was how Romy remembered him.

The Dato' had wanted a discreet background check on a potential business associate. Always useful to know if there was any dirt on the fella, that YBhg. could use as insurance for the future.

Because it would've been awkward to meet at the office, Romy was instructed to meet at the house. Somewhere in the upper reaches of Ukay Heights.

A huge-ass mansion for what, just two people? The world was so unfair.

Romy had arrived at the appointed time.

But the arrogant bastard had only rocked up in his chauffeur-driven Mercedes Benz 450 an hour later, after his golf game. And he hadn't even bothered to wear a mask.

Romy did the dude diligence as he was tasked, found nothing, the Dato' was pissed off, so that was that. Where Romy was concerned, anyway.

But as is typical, when a rich guy gets killed in his own home, it's conveniently the Indonesian maid or Nepali security guard whodunnit, especially as a pile of cash and jewelry was also missing.

In this case, it was the maid. She'd disappeared without a trace, probably back to her unpronounceable one-ojek hometown, to keep her and her extended family in bakso and kretek cigarettes indefinitely.

Romy had a vague recollection of the maid. She had been admiring what was obviously the security guard's new motorbike in the driveway. Deffo no beauty queen in her drab polyester baju kurung, her hair was scraped back into a ponytail. She had immediately assumed a servile manner when Romy mentioned his appointment with her employer and led him to cool his heels in the porch. There was something vaguely out of place about her.

But who gives a maid a second glance anyway?

Days went by after the murder of the pompous ass of a Dato'.

Suddenly, his widow seemed to be the focus of the police investigation. The netizens were up in arms.

The poor bereft Datin Harlina. She had loved her husband with her life. This outpouring of rage at the injustice of the situation, was based on a single undated photo of the Datin smiling adoringly at her husband at a charity gala event in Genting.

The police had let the Datin go after several days of intense questioning. She was astute and wealthy enough, of course, to get the most articulate lawyer to accompany her during the interrogations.

Romy glanced at his Oyster Perpetual Rolex, commonly assumed to be fake. Heck, he was just a few steps away from Petaling Street, after all.

Astonishingly, it was genuine. A gift from a grateful client. His ex-wife had wanted it to be included in their matrimonial property. But for once, his mother-in-law had taken his side and told her daughter to let him keep it.

His watch said 11.48 am.

Romy was reminded of a game he used to play with his brother when they were kids, looking forward to a cinema trip or a dinner treat at A&W.

"What's the time?"

"Guess."

"3 o'clock."

"Warm."

"3.30?"

"Too hot."

"3.15."

"Getting warmer."

"3.20?"

"Yup."

He sighed and scrolled his phone some more.

He glanced at his watch again. 11.52.

Damn. A crappy morning set to extend to a crappy –

Romy's handphone rang unexpectedly loudly in the silence of his office.

In fact, everything sounded unexpectedly loud in this new normal, with its PKPB, SOP, PUS, WFH and who knew WTF was gonna be next.

To add crème to the brûlée, this wretched midday heat probably signalled a storm brewing. Damn, it was like living in Kay Hell.

He pressed the answer button. "PI Romy."

"PI Romy?" The voice was female, slightly husky, genteel. "I'm Harlina. Datin Harlina."

The power of serendipity. Things were looking up.

There was an infinitesimal pause.

Then, "PI Romy, I have a problem."

A Datin in distress. Bring her on.

"Yes, sure, Datin," Romy beamed. "I'm here to help."

✕

Avenue J Hotel, where the husky Datin had asked to meet, was less than a two minute walk from Romy's office.

A slim building in the Art Deco style, which his ex-wife had also effused over, epitomizing elegance and geometry. Romy was slightly surprised by his client's choice of rendezvous. He'd have put her more in the Four Seasons or St. Regis category. Perhaps she was being considerate in selecting a venue close to his workplace.

The hotel, charming though its facade, and quirky its lobby meeting place, 'like having a go at the swing and gaining a new sidekick' read the mystifying tagline on its website, only mustered three stars.

Romy tapped the automated glass doors of the entrance so they slid open noiselessly, and walked briskly to the reception counter for the obligatory MySejahtera check-in and temperature record. He was beginning to get used to the drill.

He had eaten at the hotel diner a few times BC (before Covid) and was on nodding terms with the receptionist.

She inclined her head in the direction of the woman seated on the azure blue sofa.

"Datin Harlina?"

The woman, epitome of la femme fatale in a noir setting, lowered her sunglasses briefly to look at him and then slid them up again. Her designer mask matched her Diane von Furstenberg green leopard print crepe shirt dress.

But her turquoise cloth mules, with their notable sculptured heel, were obviously intended to clash with her dress, so her style came across as inimitable. Otherwise, she would have merely resembled a try-hard.

The Datin had obviously expected the place to be deserted, with the CMCO still in force. But there were other people on the opposite sofa, their classic Kanken backpacks on the ground, either waiting to check in or check out.

Romy noticed her hesitation, and it was lunchtime anyway. "We can go somewhere more private."

Romy's version of more private was his favorite café in the labyrinth of shops and eating places encased within Central Market. Four fifths of them were now closed, either temporarily or forever. All because of Covid. *Damn.*

The café of his choice was bravely bearing up but barely. It had recently undergone a name change, and the previous team of service staff was reduced to one skinny chef and a harassed-looking waitress-cum-cashier.

"The salmon beehoon soup is good." Romy was cool about lunch being on him, as he was going to slip it into his bill later on anyway, under miscellaneous expenses.

Datin Harlina shrugged gracefully and opted for the à la carte Hainanese chicken chop. She chose the cucumber juice over ice lemon tea.

Romy was having the lunch set, which came with a drink, appetizer, main and dessert.

Despite all the other tables being occupied, mainly office folk catching a quick bite, the ambience was cosy and gave off an assuring vibe of intimacy. Perhaps it was the calming effect of the tiny potted plants lined up on the walls, or the pleasing patina of the vintage furniture, or both.

But there was still that awkward silence, while waiting for their food to arrive. Romy smiled disarmingly at the Datin, hoping to draw her out of her reticence. But with her Versace shades still firmly on and her Cassey Gan mask equally firmly drawn across her face, it was akin to trying to make eye contact with a ninja.

The chicken chop saved the day.

Gracefully removing her mask in a single gesture and folding it away in her beige Chanel classic double flap bag, the Datin remarked, "I remember eating a chicken chop just like this one, as a child, at The Gap resthouse on the way up to Fraser's Hill."

This caught Romy completely by surprise. It meant he had to fast forward her age by at least ten years.

"I'm 52," she volunteered calmly.

"I'm 56," he replied, equally calmly, feeling as though he were on a hookup via a dating app, rather than a professional appointment with a client.

"I know." But she didn't proffer any explanation as to how she knew.

Instead, she took a sip of her cucumber juice and said deliberately, "PI Romy, I want you to prove I killed my husband."

Romy was so startled he choked on his beehoon. Really choked, tears streaming from his eyes, as he hacked up the offending string of beehoon which had lodged itself in his throat. It didn't augur a propitious start to their business relationship.

"Sorry, Datin. What did you say?"

Datin Harlina's face took on a slightly bored, contemptuous expression. "I said, I want you to prove I killed my husband."

To confirm the full effect of her astounding statement, she removed her sunglasses for a brief instant and Romy was able to catch a glimpse of her whole face before she slid them back on again.

"Have we met before?" enquired Romy slowly, then felt slightly silly the moment he uttered the question. After all, there had been that one widely circulated photo of her, which had gotten satu Malaysia all riled up.

Her eyes assumed a wary expression but it was so fleeting, Romy knew it had to be his imagination.

"I doubt it, PI Romy."

There was silence for several minutes as they both continued their meal.

Finally, Romy piped up. "You're serious, Datin? What's the deal?"

Datin Harlina wrinkled her rhinoplasty-enhanced Grecian nose at his bluntness. "The deal? Prove to me that I killed my husband and I'll pay you fifty thousand ringgit."

Romy's heart raced. *Fifty kay, jus' laidat!* That would nicely take care of the arrears for his loan repayment and still leave enough ringgits for a deposit on a new Bezza. Oh, and even buy Aiman a new laptop.

"But how do I do that, Datin?" The mere prospect of the possibility made Romy's voice go all squeaky.

Once more, the graceful shrug. "That's what I'm hiring you for. Prove it and you'll get the money."

"If I can't?"

"Then, no money." She hesitated slightly before continuing. "It's as straightforward as that. You have until tomorrow. I'll swing by your office at 6 pm. This is a delicate matter so I can trust you to be discreet, PI Romy? Oh, and thanks for lunch."

She rose gracefully, remembering to don her mask again as she did so, extended one Ferragamo-shod foot in front of the other and melted away.

Romy sat on in the café for some time. Actually, it was because he still had his dessert coming. Banana spring rolls, his favorite. To his disappointment, they'd run out so he had to settle for a scoop of vanilla ice cream with a squiggle of chocolate sauce. Most unsatisfactory.

But when I get my fifty kay... Romy spent an enjoyable several minutes, planning what to do with the money.

There was still that minor hurdle of fulfilling the curious task Datin had set for him, though.

Now, she was a strange one. What actually was her problem? Because if she had indeed killed her husband, as she claimed, she had already gotten away with it. As far as the police were concerned, she was no longer a suspect.

So why was it important for him, or anyone else for that matter, to prove she was the killer?

Romy ambled back to his office, deep in thought. He'd best scour the internet for every morsel of information relating to the case and piece together his own deductions.

Then he remembered his WiFi had expired. He'd have to rely on the mobile data on his phone, with its tiny screen and limited memory.

$$\times$$

It was 2 am and PI Romy hadn't gotten any closer to deducing if the wretched Datin had indeed killed her cocky ass of a husband.

He'd run through the gamut of facts surrounding the case a thousand times. It was quite straightforward.

The Dato' had been found slumped in his study, a bullet in his chest, when the police were summoned at 8 am by the security guard and driver to break down the front door. Dato' hadn't emerged from the house to go to the office at 7.45 am, as was his routine, and the maid wasn't answering the doorbell.

His murder was estimated to have taken place between 10 pm and midnight. The shot, believed to be from Dato's own gun, had been at close range. This indicated he had known the killer, as forensics had re-enacted the most plausible sequence of events leading to the murder. His gun had yet to be found.

There was no reason to suspect the security guard or the driver. They had no access into the house.

However, an Arizali beige voile kaftan belonging to the maid was found in the laundry basket, with faint traces of gunpowder residue on it. The rest of her belongings were in disarray in her room, indicating she had left in a hurry. But there could be no record of her exit on the security cameras, as they had been out of order for months.

There were also rumors afloat of the maid having previously worked in Doha and even having been, at some point, part of an elite unit of female mercenary fighters in Syria. Hence, the ease with which she handled a gun.

Romy chortled when he read that. He'd downloaded that same series on Torrent and had watched it too.

As for Datin Harlina, she was on a staycation at MO that fateful night, the driver having dropped her off there earlier in the day. Datin was known to the concierge staff, having often stayed there, in her own words, "to recharge my batteries."

Several other hotel staff were also able to vouch for her throughout her stay, as she had been seen in various areas of the hotel such as the spa and bistro.

Around the estimated time of the murder, a supper of organic chicken congee and camomile tea was being delivered to her suite. The F&B manager, who brought up the tray personally, admitted to not actually seeing the Datin when he entered the suite. But he could hear the waves splashing in the whirlpool in the bathroom.

And he was certain it was Datin Harlina in there because just a few minutes earlier, she had spoken to him on the in-house phone: "I'll leave the door ajar. Just put the tray on the table, thank you."

Then it came to the morning after the murder. Two police officers came to the hotel to break the sad news to the Datin, who was enjoying a leisurely breakfast of blueberry oatmeal waffles and a tofu omelette at the Mosaic restaurant.

The female police officer had related in hushed tones, "Datin Harlina punya terkejut, sampai hampir pengsan, tau! Kesian Datin."

If the police had their suspicions as to why they decided to refocus their investigations on the Datin, their reasons were not revealed.

The security guard and driver were questioned yet again. Their testimonies remained intact and there was no reason to doubt them.

The security guard though, had repeated, "Kesian itu Datin. Pembantu rumah slalu mau lari. Kesian itu Datin."

The driver had echoed in a similar vein, "Datin baik. Ada kalanya, Datin sendiri yang kemas rumah. Kesian dia. Dato' tu, memang jenis ganas, ada angin."

Romy tossed and turned on his tatami mat. Trust his ex-wife to have had the foresight to take their Ikea Hafslo sprung mattress with frame and headboard with her when she moved out.

But once that fifty kay was in his bank account...

What was that phrase which kept cropping up in the case? "Kesian Datin."

Strange how she was made out to be the victim, rather than the luckless Dato'. The perks of being a beautiful woman.

Romy pulled out his phone again to scour for any other photos circulating on the internet of the Datin.

She was notoriously private. No social media accounts which Romy could call on his tech-savvy pals to hack into for a fee. He chanced on one or two occasional pics of her in *Tatler* and *Prestige*. But she was always looking away from the camera.

Then again, old money was like that. It was only the new rich, especially the ones selling their own brand of cosmetics or headscarves, who had this misplaced sense of entitlement, constantly caterwauling to be noticed.

At 4.35 am, PI Romy finally drifted into a dreamless sleep.

6.44 am, his phone rang.

"When are you ordering Aiman's laptop?"

"Today is a good day," Romy mumbled in a beatific tone.

Was it? He still hadn't the foggiest how he was going to prove to his client that she was the villain who'd bumped off her pompous bastard of a husband.

That fifty grand, so near, seemed to be getting away.

Another Grab ride to the office.

Ah, but once I get my new Bezza...

A man can dream.

His clerk was in. A severe-looking woman in a faded lilac tudung Ariani with soft awning. It was obvious she neither liked her job nor Romy.

Romy was indifferent to her. She cost him little in wages and didn't talk much, which fulfilled his expectations.

So he was somewhat perplexed when he once had a spooky wet dream about her. In fact, it freaked him out so much that he had to leave town for a week on the pretext of an outstation matter.

"WiFi not working, Encik Romy. How to send emails?"

"Tomorrow all will be good," replied Romy flippantly.

The atmosphere in the dingy office felt suddenly oppressive. He got up abruptly and went out.

$$\times$$

Datin Harlina sounded slightly breathless. "PI Romy, I'm afraid I'll be late. My salsa class was extended."

"Take your time, Datin," said Romy courteously.

"How are your investigations going?" she enquired sweetly. Even through the phone waves, she could still exude a sensuous charm.

"Oh, it's going great guns," replied Romy heartily. He didn't get why there was a sudden giggle from the Datin. Then again, women were sometimes just weird laidat.

He wished the meeting could be tomorrow, as for the life of him, damnit, he still couldn't figure it out. But he'd just give it his best shot anyway, hazard a guess. *Wang besar, wang besar.*

It was past 7 pm when Datin Harlina appeared, still in her salsa gear.

Her claret red ruched Maria Lucia Hohan dress and Manolo Blahnik satin stilettos screamed sensuality and seduction. There was a luminosity about her, an almost unearthly aura.

Despite the aircon having already been turned off an hour ago, a chill hung in the air.

It was also the first time Romy was able to contemplate her whole face, sans sunglasses and mask, at leisure. Slowly, she shook her hair back in a languorous gesture.

She looked at Romy slightly challengingly before lowering her eyelids, glittery in Pat McGrath's signature Celestial Divinity eyeshadow.

Romy stared back at her. Where was it that he had seen – *her earrings!* That was it, her Buccellati diamond earrings! And the subservient yet faintly mocking expression as she lowered her eyes.

It came back to him. That afternoon at the Dato's house. The maid who had been hanging around the front entrance. He had assumed it was the maid because she'd been holding a broom.

It had been Datin Harlina herself.

What was it the security guard had said? And the driver? Romy racked his brains to remember.

Ah yes. "Ada kalanya, Datin sendiri yang kemas rumah."

The earrings were the giveaway. The 'maid' had been wearing them.

And the "Kesian Datin." Repeated once too often by the security guard, in the tone of one who could be described as… lovestruck?

Damn. Why had it never occurred to him? Of course, the security guard and the Datin! What a cliché.

Likewise, who would have noticed when she slipped out of the hotel into the night, in the aptly nondescript kaftan she later discarded, to the security guard and his Yamaha NVX waiting round the corner.

The Datin spoke first. "So you know."

"I do," Romy's reply sounded incongruous, even to his own ears. Such a phrase was usually preceded by "Till death do us part."

She sighed and took out her phone. "What are your account details? I'll do an online transfer."

In a daze, Romy told her. He checked his account to be sure the money was in. It was. The rich weren't bound by such frivolous bank rules as a daily transfer limit.

There was a swift movement on the stairs. *Oh, but she hadn't come alone.* The security guard had tagged along too.

Datin Harlina sighed again, apologetically this time. "If only you hadn't come to the house that day. You do understand, PI Romy. We can't take any chances."

The guard was aiming a pistol at Romy. But out of habit, Romy never went anywhere without what he affectionately called his baby G. And two decades of active service in the army had made him the most proficient sharpshooter in his regiment.

There was a single shot.

Romy replaced his Glock 19 neatly in its holster at his waist and replied smoothly, "Indeed, Datin. We can't."

2

✕

PI ROMY & THE
CIRQUE DU SOLEK

✕

PI Romy bounded up the triple flight of stairs to his office with a spring in his step.

Life was good.

- He'd bought a new car. ✓
- He'd treated his son Aiman to a new laptop. ✓
- He was up to date with the bank loan for his apartment. ✓
- Heck, he'd even ordered his ex-wife a bouquet of stargazer lilies from Flower Chimp for her birthday. ✓

His good cheer was as infectious as the Covid thingy – his normally dour-faced clerk was actually smiling.

"Encik Romy, I'm getting married," she told him coyly.

Romy was not unchivalrous enough to gasp in astonishment. But his felicitations were perhaps a little too effusive to sound genuine.

"Why not take the day off!" he exclaimed enthusiastically. "I'm sure you have plenty to prepare."

His clerk simpered and protested feebly, "No, no, it's okay."

But she was already logging off her computer and gathering up her new Bonia handbag (present from fiancé?) while Romy was in mid-sentence.

The office suddenly felt eerily quiet after she left.

PI Romy glanced in the direction of the entrance and was immediately reminded of a recent unpleasantness. Not one of his prouder moments, as he truly abhorred violence. But his action, as he kept reminding himself, had been in self-defense.

Then, there had been the business of disposing the body. The Datin mastermind had maintained her cool throughout and hadn't batted an eyelid when Romy had quoted his price, or what he'd tactfully referred to as "arranging for pickup."

Well, one couldn't exactly just order a Grab to chauffeur a corpse across town at eight o'clock in the evening.

Fortuitously, there had been other numbers Romy could call and he picked the most reliable one, which naturally proved the most expensive.

Romy shivered involuntarily. Despite a week having gone by since the mishap, he still had the heebie-jeebies, especially when he heard footsteps up the stairs.

Wait, what was that… there *were* footsteps echoing up the stairs.

The lady who entered the office was young, late twenties at most. There was a Parisienne air about her. Perhaps it was the jaunty, mustard – colored beret. Or the monogrammed scarf tied in a hasty knot on the handle of her small St. Laurent leather satchel.

If Romy's ex-wife were present, she would have been swift to correct him. "That's not a scarf, 'My. It's a twilly."

The young woman hesitated in the doorway and adjusted her beret.

"May I come in?"

PI Romy was intrigued. Only an atas person would use the verb "May". Plebs and proles would just say "Can".

His reply was equally atas, thanks to his English-language teacher ex-wife. "Certainly, you may."

"I believe someone's trying to kill me, PI Romy." La 'demoiselle was understandably in an agitated state.

Romy sighed inwardly but outwardly adopted a patient tone. "I think this is a matter for the Police, Cik – er –"

"Inaya. Puteri Inaya. No, PI Romy," Mademoiselle was emphatic. "I cannot engage the police in this matter. You see, the person attempting to murder me is one of my BFFs."

Romy didn't get it. "Ya, but if she's trying to kill you –"

"Oh, PI Romy, you must understand. I cannot openly accuse one of my best friends of attempted murder. Especially when I can't be sure whom amongst them it is."

There again, the atas manner of speech. "Whom" rather than "who", "amongst" instead of "among".

PI Romy was firm. "I'm sorry, Cik – er – Cik Puteri."

"Name your price," she trilled sweetly.

Romy did.

He wished he'd added another few kay to his five-figure price as the Pute briskly placed a six-inch wad of banknotes on the table.

"Here's half. The balance to be paid once you've identified the culprit."

"But how would I go about –"

She wrote rapidly on a sheet of The Westin KL notepaper.

"I'm hosting a cosy girly lunch at home tomorrow. My besties – the suspects – they'll all be there."

She looked at him appraisingly.

"Come as the butler. I'm short-staffed. My Nepali houseboy took off last week, claiming he'd lost his brother. So careless of him."

$$\times$$

The details provided by his new client were scanty.

She had scribbled her address and the names of the suspects, four in all, on the paper she'd handed him.

Perhaps 'scribbled' was an understatement. Her handwriting was practically illegible. Romy wondered where she'd gone to school. Or, if indeed she had gone to school.

1. Fatto Farfalla
2. Tinker Amanott
3. Fatim Haia Safie
4. Daun Serai Inina

A quick Google search yielded nothing, until Romy realized that the names were actually Dato' Farhana, Tengku Amaryllis, Datin Hana Sofia and Puan Sri Irina.

Probably, his ex-wife would have screeched excitedly in recognition at these indubitably illustrious-sounding names. But all Romy could think was, who the hell were these people?

He checked out various news portals and was rewarded by a plethora of effusive features and interviews, extolling their beauty, dedication to charitable causes and remarkable business acumen (in that order).

One facetious news reporter had conveniently coined the quintet, Le Cirque du Solek, in reference to the vast cosmetics empire they owned jointly. Which, if it were to be believed, they had started as a side hustle in their school days. (One news portal even mentioned kindergarten.)

Stalking their social media also yielded reams of posts. Every morsel of their have-have lives was gloated over for the have-nots to eat their hearts out.

Romy felt quite fatigued after merely reading the daily 8 things they did before 8 am.

It was as though they had been conjoined at birth.

They'd all lived in the same affluent neighborhood, attended the same fancy school (Ah, so the good Puteri had indeed gone to school), even left for the UK together to further their studies.

To Romy's surprise, the bimbo-looking Pute had actually trained as a doctor at Imperial. So that probably accounted for the illegible handwriting.

Dato' Farhana, despite her doe eyes and waif-like expression turned out to be an LSE alumnus, specializing in international mergers and acquisitions.

Appropriately bespectacled but fashionably so, Tengku Amaryllis (Amy) had graduated from Cambridge (the illustrious England one, not its near-namesake in the US). In Biochemistry, no less, specializing in molecular genetics.

Unspectacled but equally fashionably so, Datin Hana Sofia had also been at Cambridge, reading Philosophy, with a keen interest in axiology.

A photo of them both, punting at dawn on the River Cam in their hand-beaded Salabianca evening gowns, tended to surface as the top image on any online search.

Apparently, as they giggled confidingly to a reporter, they'd only attended university because it sounded like it would be a blast, "and Trinity College held amaze-balls." Romy, understandably, didn't get the pun.

Puan Sri Irina – nicknamed 'Bubbles' but it was never revealed how or why – appeared to be the only underachiever of the circle. She had embarked on a Psychology course at London Metropolitan University but abandoned it halfway to marry.

But oh, what a catch! Okay, so Tan Sri was no spring chicken and had a serious hair deficit. But the surplus in his bank balance more than made up for any of his shortcomings.

Not to be outdone, it was just a matter of time before the others reeled in their own, rollin' husbands. But unlike Bubbles, who seemed genuinely fond of her old man, from the way she clung to him in photos, they soon tired of theirs.

The saucy shenanigans attached to their respective divorce proceedings put rice on the table for the press reporters for weeks.

The Puteri's had been particularly vitriolic.

An unexpected outburst of unbridled abuse had emanated from her spurned spouse outside the courtroom. Someone recorded it and it went viral.

Netizens made a martyr of her.

It helped that she was looking very vulnerable in her Queen Rania of Jordan-inspired, silk wrap abaya. Shielding her face with her ringless (save for a solitary Mappin & Webb eternity band), beautifully tapered hands, she stoically faced the invectives slung at her by her previously smitten-till-he-claimed-he-got bitten, ex-husband.

Romy read on, transfixed.

Then, he realized it was already nearly noon and he had yet to pick out an attire appropriate for the occasion. Damn, if he didn't set off soon, he was going to be late.

He went through his sparse wardrobe to decide which would most resemble a butler's uniform. In the end, he chose a white shirt and a pair of slate gray trousers. But there was just something very waiter-like about his ensemble, a butler being in Romy's estimation a couple of steps up the service ladder.

As an afterthought, he slipped on a jacquard waistcoat with botanical accents, for a dash of panache.

The Pute lived in the penthouse unit of a cluster of condominiums in Kenny Hills.

Once consisting only of graceful bungalows dotted sporadically all over the said bukit, a populist Datuk Bandar had advocated the construction of stratified residences. Because as he announced flippantly, let's also give the pariahs a chance lah, to own homes in high-class areas.

Luckily for the plain-speaking DB, it was before the age of internet vigilantism.

Security at Seri Tinggi Towers was tight, as expected. But the guards were courteous, especially as Romy cut an almost dashing figure at the wheel of his new Bezza, with his waistcoat.

"Okeh, *Ma'am*, I'm here," he said to the Pooter, by way of greeting. Posh surroundings tended to make him gauche.

Too late, he noticed his snazzy waistcoat matched the tablecloth.

But La Pute was enchanted. "PI Romy, how astute of you! My theme today is 'Tropical Garden'." She was indeed resplendent in a Jovian Mandagie modern kebaya with floral and leaf motifs.

Romy grinned ingratiatingly. "Erm, ya. So how do you want me to help with the guests? Maybe, check on the food?" Frankly, he had no idea as to his duties.

Poot's reply was vague. "Don't fret, PI Romy. My houseboy came back. Oh, ditsy me! I forgot. You're meant to be the butler, right? Well then, just buttle on, darling."

He hung about deferentially by the jade and gold-embellished Belle Époque screen along one side of the room, feeling more self-conscious than ever.

Each guest floated in within two minutes of the other, just enough time to slip off their masks for a flurry of kisses and a meaningless exchange of greetings.

Doll-sized designer handbags, which could barely hold a lipstick, appeared to be the current 'must have' accessory.

Lunch was already laid out in exquisite oversized Orrefors crystal platters along the center of the bespoke Boca Do Lobo dining table.

Romy stood by quietly, observing the obligatory rush to snap photos of the fabulously presented food.

He was not at all impressed by the comestibles themselves, though. The carefully curated menu resembled something goats might enjoy. But it was obviously how the girlies managed to stay super slim.

Still, there was a tray of confectionery on the shagreen JP Meunier console, which looked more promising. Ah yes, of course. The girlies would need to earn their portion by munching on the greens first.

"Waiter," one of them, Datin Hana Sofia, or Confucius, as Romy privately referred to her (his list of philosophers was exclusively male and extremely limited), languidly handed him her iPhone.

Romy was momentarily nonplussed before realizing she wanted photos to be taken, "over lunch, hun. For the 'Gram."

"If you don't mind, Datin Con-fu, er..." Romy found it a problem taking his eyes off the generous décolletage of her exquisitely hand-painted iKartini silk blouse. "I'll take with my phone and send to you."

An indifferent swish of her glossy blow-curled tresses indicated agreement.

The girlies had, between giggles, decided to observe social distancing at the lunch table and adjusted their place settings so they sat very demurely apart from each other.

Poot sat at the head, Bubbles on her right, Dato' Farhana (Romy codenamed her Bambi) on her left. Tengku Amy was at the other end, Confucius on her right.

"Darling, there's a place set for you too," purred la Puteri, in hostess with the mostest mode.

Romy thought, erroneously, as it turned out, that she was referring to her Savannah cat, which was filing its claws on an Hermès Avalon throw blanket.

This was awkward. He had never in his life lunched on his own with a group of ladies. *Damn.* He felt almost obliged to cross his legs and titter behind his shirt cuff.

They didn't seem to think it singular to include him in their party.

He had, though, overheard Tengku Amy, on discovering he was to be seated at her side, murmur to her hostess, "So who's the shy dude?"

"Oh, just my coy boy, darling."

To his relief, they largely ignored him, except when they wanted photos taken, "for the 'Gram, hun."

"Be sure you only take pics of me from a side angle," cautioned Bubbles.

She was acutely conscious of still being a kilo away from her pre-natal weight, despite having had her child four years ago. She even had a constant hashtag #meinkampf on her social media account, highlighting her weight issues, 'my struggle is Real, dearies.'

Romy obsequiously assured her he would take note.

The high society conversation, as expected, revolved round high snobiety.

But despite the free-flowing carafes of sangria at each end of the table, the girlies remained in high sobriety.

Romy soaked in the arty chit-chat, the insatiable appetite for conspicuous consumerism, the clarion call for diversity and inclusion, and the erudite arguments for combating black swan events.

He couldn't comprehend their abhorrence of the last, though. He'd been to a few black-tie events in the past, which he'd thoroughly enjoyed. Probably, making a fashion statement with a swan theme was tricky.

He also made a mental observation that beneath the wafer-thin veneer of chummy sisterly exchange of ('kay, tell) confidences, there were undercurrents of… discontent? Rivalry? But that was totally to be expected when it came to a bunch of women. No, it was something deeper. Evil.

The aircon suddenly blew an icy gust of air. Romy felt his spine tingle.

The Tengku announced shyly that she was getting engaged to her new-found love. Their whirlwind on / off courtship had been the focus of social media attention for many months. There was no mistaking her joy.

The Poot was especially ecstatic. "That's totes awesome, darling!" she squealed. And then whispered in a bored tone to Bambi beside her, inadvertently loud enough for Romy to hear, "Actually, she called to tell me this last week."

More sangria flowed.

Romy primly poured himself a goblet of sparkling water from the crystal decanter and sipped it slowly.

He tried his best to enjoy the food on his plate. But spiralized zucchini and avocado salad in a pesto dressing just wasn't his thing. It was a relief when the houseboy, seeing his discomfiture, discreetly removed his still-full plate.

"Dessert! Made by my own fair hands!" announced their hostess, as she took the tray of Portmeirion bowls from the console and laid one before each guest.

Each small bowl was initialed. La Pute was a gracious hostess. There was even one with an 'R' for Romy.

Romy was familiar with desserts and pastries, thanks to his ex-wife.

"Baking mad you are," he'd grumbled when, heavily pregnant with Aiman, she persisted in slaving over a hot oven. At the time, she was attempting to perfect Nigella Lawson's strawberry pavlova recipe.

He didn't get it when she unexpectedly gave him an almost affectionate pinch on the cheek. "You can be so witty, 'My."

But these bits and pieces arranged higgledy-piggledy in a bowl? They contained the obligatory staples of crisp meringue, whipped cream and strawberries, true.

Unfortunately, in Romy's view, the results looked akin to the jigsaw killer in *Saw* having taken liberties with poor Puteri's creation.

Romy eyed his Pavlova gone wrong, gingerly. However there were squeals of pure pleasure from all the other guests.

"Eton mess!" exclaimed Bambi joyfully.

"To die for!" declared Bubbles, as she playfully grabbed Pooter's bowl and set it beside her own.

"Hey, see the 'P' there, that's mine!" protested Poot.

"Too bad," giggled Bubbles, as she devoured both bowls at the same time.

"A moment on your lips, a lifetime on your hips," quipped la Puteri, as a parting shot.

She dragged her chair round to the other end of the table to chat with TA and Conf.

Romy positioned himself to get a shot of Bubbles' unashamed gluttony. Bubbles obliged with an exaggerated gesture of seraphic bliss.

Romy returned to his seat and tentatively popped a spoonful of the gooey meringue mixture in his mouth. It tasted surprisingly good.

He glanced across. One second, Bubbles was talking and laughing with Bambi. The next, she was choking and gasping for breath.

"Water," she whimpered, leaning forward lengthways to reach for the decanter.

Bambi desperately poured water down Bubbles' throat and hit her repeatedly on the back.

Conf and TA remained frozen and looked on at the spectacle with a horrified fascination.

La Pute forgot all about being a gracious hostess, much less that she was a trained medic. Her panic-stricken, blood-curdling scream was enough to have persuaded Dracula a change of diet would be good.

Romy was the only one who had the presence of mind to holler to them to call Emergency services. After which, he tried to apply the Heimlich maneuver and then CPR on the, by now, limp Bubbles, to no avail.

There was nothing stuck in her throat. Her airways appeared clear. She had no known allergies, no medical history of epilepsy or similar.

It turned out that Bubbles had been harboring an abdominal aortic aneurysm, known only to herself and their girly Cirque du Solek.

Even her inconsolable husband had been unaware of her secret ailment.

As the distraught Puteri, who was the self-appointed spokesperson (well, Bubbz did die in her house) sobbed, "She didn't want to stress out poor Tan Sri. Especially as he's already so very old."

It was clear that the Pavlova Penyet with its lashings of cholesterol-laden clotted cream had proven too much for Bubbles' dicky heart.

$$\times$$

A couple of days later, Romy and Puteri were touching base at the Chow Kit Kitchen & Bar.

Romy was savoring the juniper and vanilla notes in his KL Hustle, which one drinks critic had described as 'too much fun not to order'.

Prior to that, he'd had a couple of Swettenham sundowners because, well, it was already that time of day. They were on the Poot's tab, anyways.

Chastely nursing a virgin piña colada, the Pute had substituted her perky beret for a Bokitta Voila maxi hijab.

"PI Romy, you do see that it couldn't possibly have been the cause, don't you?" There was a faint plea in her voice.

"What couldn't have been the cause?" Romy's deliberate obtuseness was often effective in drawing people out.

But the recent traumatic event had made Puteri circumspect. "Bubbles' aneurism, as the cause of death."

She continued patiently. "It was just a tiny one, the minutest hiatal hernia. I was with her at the London Heart Clinic on Wimpole Street when she was diagnosed, just before the lockdown in March. Thank God we didn't have to quarantine when we got back." The Pute's relief was genuine and heartfelt.

She lowered her voice dramatically, "Bubba was poisoned, I'm sure of it."

Romy said dreamily, as he made a mental estimation of the quantity of fermented grape juice in his drink. "You think so? By one of the others at lunch?"

Puteri's lower lip quivered. "PI Romy, I'm scared."

Romy took a yam cracker from the bowl on the table and nibbled it thoughtfully. His mind was still pleasurably hazy. "But we all ate the same thing."

The Pute said slowly, "My Eton mess. I didn't get to have any. Bubbles ate mine."

"But Cik Puteri, you announced yourself that you made it," Romy pointed out.

Her reply was understandably defensive. "And I did. It was on the console that whole time. One of the others could have slipped a vial of – of cyanide into my bowl. Three milligrams would suffice to be fatal. And no one would be any the wiser."

Romy knew that was the beauty of cyanide poisoning. It was difficult to diagnose. It was also unlikely Bubbles' body could be exhumed to find out. There was no reason.

"And I found this. Look inside it."

She delved into her Rive Gauche checked tote and handed him a miniscule brown bag with a chain strap.

Romy recognized it as one of the girlies' handbags at lunch. He took out an exquisitely shaped vial and unscrewed its turret-like crown cap.

"It's just a lipstick," he said. "Made by some person called Christian Lou – Lou –?"

"Louboutin," Puteri interrupted. "No, not that thingy. The other container."

Romy felt inside the bag again, which yielded a tiny pill box encrusted with jewels in the shape of a flower. He prized it open to find powdery white crumbs.

"Cyanide pills." Poot was on the verge of breaking down. "I'm a doctor. I know."

"The motif on the bag says F," Romy observed, astutely so he thought. "F for Farhana."

"That's the Fendi motif," snapped Puteri crossly. She could not believe Romy's ignorance.

She shoved the cover of the pill box almost into his face. "Recognize the flower?"

"Lily?" Romy hazarded a guess. "Yes, a lily," he repeated, sounding more sure of himself.

"The light's on but nobody's home," murmured Puteri.

"Have you met with the other ladies since the funeral?" Romy abruptly changed the subject, as he returned the contents into the bag and placed it beside him.

She shook her head and fiddled sadly with the magnetic pin on her hijab. "Only on FaceTime. I'm nervous about going out anywhere." She looked furtively over her shoulder. "I have this feeling I'm being followed."

Then, a thought occurred to her. "Have *you* seen any of the girlies?"

Romy was at the beatific stage of his imbibitions when his inhibitions were lowered. Neither was his frame of mind very lucid.

"We have, um, exchanged a couple of calls," he remarked expansively. He wanted to add that the caller had ranted a lot of bull, all of which Romy had already read about, before.

But the Poot butting in sharply with a "Whom d'you mean by 'we'?" threw him off-kilter.

"Don'ch bark." Romy's speech was getting slurry. "You sound like my ex-wife."

With a supreme effort, he brushed off the flecks of the yam cracker from his shirt front and enunciated his words as grandly as he could. "Gather the girlies at your plaishe tomorrow. I'll vereal the murdererer then."

$$\times$$

Romy awoke the next morning with a pounding headache. The sensation was akin to Muhammad Ali having somehow floated inside his brain to use it to practice the rapid-fire left jabs for which he was famous.

Romy got out of bed cautiously in a single movement and it was as though Ali had thrown one of his 'snake licks' straight into the center of Romy's parietal lobe.

Things improved slightly after his second cup of coffee.

But when he went to the basement spot where his new Bezza was parked, his heart missed a beat. It wasn't there.

Then he remembered his little bender of the previous evening. He'd prudently left his car with the valet and Grabbed it home. Luckily, the nearest stop for The Chow Kit was on his train route.

The walk to Sentul LRT station did wonders for his throbbing head.

For the thousandth time, as the fervent public service announcements to beware of pickpockets and to stand clear of the train doors resonated right through the innermost part of his cerebrum, Romy swore he was going to stay on the wagon, once and for all. The ironic timing of his statement completely escaped him.

There was a mother with her two little sons seated opposite him in the carriage. The elder one proudly clutched a Hot Wheels car. Romy was reminded of his Aiman at that age.

The train veered slightly and the younger boy bumped his head against the window.

"Ow! Mak, Abang buat!" he yelped.

"Brape kali Mak dah cakap, jangan asyik menyakat Adik!" The exasperated mother snatched the toy from Abang and kept it away in her bag.

Adik smirked. The same scenario had probably played countless times before, because the guiltless Abang merely hung his head and looked resigned.

Romy gave him a sympathetic smile, which elicited a protective glare from Mak. She'd read how pedophiles stalked their prey on public transport.

At the office, his clerk was already there, clacking away on the computer keys.

She beamed genially at him in greeting, like an air hostess aboard a Malaysia Airlines flight. It was obvious she was still on cloud nine. Romy wasn't sure he liked the new her.

The morning went by very slowly, especially as Romy's throbbing head meant that the slightest noise seemed to reverberate like the pendulum ride at Genting theme park. He had hated it but his son Aiman thought the ride was totes cool.

$$\times$$

The houseboy admitted Romy into the study of Puteri's, by – now, almost-familiar home.

Romy was surprised to find the girlies already present.

Even in the depths of their mourning, photo opportunities could not be dispensed with. He almost expected them to start a live stream.

The Poot hadn't thought to inform them beforehand, as to the reason for the gathering.

Not unreasonably, as it was just after Friday prayers and Romy had forgotten to remove his kopiah, they assumed he was coming to give a khutbah.

Still solicitous about the new normal, they elected to sit in different areas of the room.

Bambi chose a Churchill leather button-backed armchair and absentmindedly twirled a few tendrils of hair, which had escaped from her silk dUck monogram scarf.

TA draped herself on the plush velvet daybed and watched the diamonds on her Van Cleef & Arpels Frivole ring dance in the afternoon light.

Confucius, fittingly, sat on the mahogany library step stool by the magnificent floor-to-ceiling bookcase, which was crammed with medical books. She pulled one out and frowned at its cover.

La Puteri leaned against her antique Mazarin bureau famously bought at auction from Sotheby's, and nervously arranged and rearranged her collection of Montblanc fountain pens.

Romy introduced himself formally in a ta daa! manner. There was a polite flicker of interest.

But when he embarked on the purpose of his presence, the atmosphere changed perceptibly. Each of them involuntarily drew defensively a little closer to themselves.

Confucius roused herself from desultorily turning the pages of a graphically illustrated book on sexually transmissible diseases. "I'm confused. You're claiming one of us wants Pooters dead but killed Bubbles with cyanide by mistake!" she exclaimed incredulously.

Romy replied with a smarmy little bow. "Indeed, Datin. It would appear so."

Bambi giggled nervously and addressed Puteri. "If this is one of your jokes, Sweetie –"

"It isn't a joke!" La Pute exclaimed hysterically.

TA stopped playing with her ring and undraped herself from the daybed to sit upright. "So whom among us is the culprit? I take it the murderer has to be one of us?"

Romy produced her Fendi mini baguette bag with a flourish. He took out the pill box and showed its contents. "Cyanide pills."

"That's my bag," admitted TA. "I must've left it here the other day."

"And the little container," added Romy smoothly. "Note the floral design on it."

"An amaryllis lily!" Pooters burst out.

Confucius stifled a ladylike scream.

There was a stunned silence as everyone took in the information.

"Oh my God, Amy!" Bambi was aghast.

"Murderer!" shrieked Confucius, forgetting to be ladylike.

"What!? No, I swear it wasn't me!" TA shouted un-grammatically, unminding her English in her zeal to deny her guilt. "Besides, that's not my pill box."

"Liar! I've seen that container on your dressing table," snapped Puteri.

"It was in your handbag, Tengku, " Romy reminded TA.

"It's NOT my pill box," Her Highness declared vehemently. "And where would I get cyanide pills from, anyway? They're hardly an item one can source on Shopee."

"You're a chemist," Confucius reminded her scornfully.

Puteri covered her face with her hands. "Why would you want to kill me, Amy? You're evil."

Romy watched for several moments. Poot was reduced completely to tears as her two besties clucked and fussed over her, while the hapless TA merely hung her head and said nothing.

His train of thought chugged along in a completely different direction. His conversations with the caller, whose identity Puteri had been so keen to know.

Train... Abang and Adik on his LRT ride that morning.

Just in time, Romy experienced an epiphany. *Puti mak engkau!*

When he finally spoke, it was slowly and deliberately. "Tengku Amaryllis, you're not evil."

He swung round to the Pute. "Cik Puteri Inaya, *you* are. You're the one who killed Bubb –er, Puan Sri Irina. You hated arwah Puan Sri because she was happily married and had a child.

Two things you long for most in your life. And you hate Tengku Amy too. Because she seems to have found true happiness in her new love. You just can't stand to see people happy, can you, Puteri Inaya? You never have. God knows how you managed to – er – contain your hate all these years. I watched that viral video of your ex-husband's. All he said about you is indeed true. Right down to your fertility issues and obsessing about other people's blessings instead of counting your own. You knew Puan Sri would eat your dessert. It's a standing joke between you both. Even captioned on your Instagram again and again, when you lunch together. The recent exchange of calls I mentioned to you yesterday, they were between your ex-husband and myself. He'd been having his staff follow you, as he knew you were up to no good."

Romy forbore to mention that the 'call a spade a spade' of a Dato' had bluntly hollered down the phone, "What would that bitch want with a cheapskate lau ya detective like you? She's just using you to cover her backside for some sick plan of hers."

Instead, he rephrased it in more refined terms, which would have made his ex-wife proud. "You hired me as a smokescreen. Cik Puteri Inaya, no one is trying to kill you."

Then, straightening his kopiah, Romy addressed the others. "I'm done here. Up to the rest of you, how you want to avenge arwah Puan Sri's death. But if I know you girlies, you'll come up with an appropriate punishment, far worse than any punishment handed down by a court of law."

He paused and added as an afterthought. "Oh ya, Cik Puteri, just one last thing. If I can have the balance fifty percent you owe me for identifying 'the culprit', please. Online transfer is fine."

3

✕

PI ROMY & THE BASHFUL BILLIONAIRE

✕

PI Romy disliked receiving calls from his brother.

It was personal.

Irfan, older than Romy by three years, had obviously won the genetic lottery. Or the mould was broken after he was born. Or the hospital had screwed up and Irfan wasn't actually his biological brother.

Whatever.

"'My? So how's everything, 'dik?" The invariable nasal whine in his brother's patronizing tone reminded Romy how much he couldn't stand the bugger.

"Laidat lah."

That should've sufficed to kill any further convo but Irfan could never take the hint.

Or perhaps, Romy thought to his surprise, *Abang might, for once, have landed himself in a tight spot.*

Romy waited.

"'My, I'm in deep shit, man. You have to help me."

Wait, what? My hotshot goody-two-shoes Abang, aka Mak's golden boy, needing my help?

This was great!

Romy tried unsuccessfully to hide the smirk in his voice, while sounding solicitous at the same time. "Oh ya? What happened, 'bang?"

"Someone's blackmailing me. And uhh, well, yeah…"

"Okayy…" Romy examined his fingernails and waited some more.

"So… erm… I admit I er… well, I'm hoping you can nego for me."

Romy had always known his brother was a dungu. Yep, smart but also a dungu.

"No point, 'bang. The bastard will just bleed you dry, then expose you. Better to make a police report." He added virtuously for good measure. "Whatever you did, mesti ada hikmah di sebaliknya."

Actually, Romy didn't know what wisdom could possibly be derived from the consequence of his brother's indiscretions.

But it sounded good. And preachy.

God only knew, Irfan had preached enough in the past about Romy's misdemeanors.

"It's complicated," his Abang sighed.

Romy's lips twitched. Wasn't it always.

"I'll come over now and explain?"

Romy glanced at the digital clock beside him. Almost midnight. And he was nicely tucked up in bed, munching peria crispy and enjoying a slow-burn horror movie, *Suraya* on Astro Boo. He was about to say, "Can't it wait till tomorrow?" when the desperate note in his brother's voice struck a chord. "'Kay."

There was no tidying up necessary to make the place presentable.

Romy was a minimalist. Not to mention, his apartment space was as premium as leg room on a long-haul Air Asia flight.

Damnit, would the era of Air Asia long-haul flights ever return?. That reboot of his favorite boyhood police procedural set in Hawaii, which he was watching just before *Suraya*... suddenly, he had a hankering to visit Honolulu, of all places. The actress playing the rookie officer Kono Kalakaua reminded him of his secondary school crush.

Or the Maldives. One of his former cohorts when they were part of the UN 'Operation Reliance' was always asking, *when you come visit my country, man? Don't wait a hundred years.*

Yeah, if only. Maldives had the best dive sites and his Aiman would deffo be bowled over by the manta rays and whale sharks.

The buzz of his front door brought him out of his wishful thinking with a jolt.

Holy shit, Abang had definitely hit 190 in his Mazda MX-5. It was normally a forty minute drive from his bourgie residence in Setia Alam to Sentul.

Sitting himself down without ceremony on Romy's shabby Fella Design armchair, his normally calm and composed brother sounded like a basket case.

"I didn't do it. Swear to God. Someone set me up. Azreen was already dead when I got there."

"Azreen??" Romy's interest was piqued. This was a side of Abang he never knew.

He let Irfan blather on wildly in his high little voice, savoring every morsel of Mister Goody Two Shoes' anguish.

"Omaigod. Clubbed to death. By my big Bertha."

A crime of passion! Romy envisioned a well-endowed, dusky woman wielding a golf stick. But big Bertha turned out to be the name of a line of golf clubs.

"I thought I'd just misplaced it a while ago but it must have been stolen."

Slowly, Romy was able to put the pieces of the story together.

Irfan was an avid golfer. Such a chi-chi game, in Romy's view. But it was useful in his brother's line of work as a wealth investment consultant.

He had various sets of golf kakis, which meant being active in different chat groups.

So there was the Hole-some group, who played for health and exercise.

Then there was the tiga suku group. Because their tee-off time was at 3.15pm.

Another group was the Hole-y Ones. Very exclusive, as only those who had scored a hole in one could be added to the group.

Finally, there was an even more exclusive-than-thou group, going by the initials TBTM.

It was apparently TBTM which was the thorn in his brother's backside.

"TBTM?" Romy hadn't the foggiest what the letters stood for. "Ya, so?"

Irfan drew in a deep breath. "It's short for Talk Birdie To Me."

"Ya, so?" Romy was beginning to sound like a parrot.

Irfan groaned. What kind of dungu detective was his adik?

"What d'ya think, 'My? That we actually geddidup in the bunker by watching sparrows and sun birds flitting overhead?"

Romy felt a sliver of peria crispy stuck between his back molars and sucked in his teeth thoughtfully, as he digested what his brother was saying. He could hardly believe his ears.

"But it's all online, right? And you go by a moniker."

Romy was quite pleased with his usage of the last word. He'd learnt it from Aiman.

Irfan hesitated. "Not always online." His next words came out in a rush. "Sometimes we hook up. Uhh, there is – well, was – this erm… junior caddy. Azreen. We got close."

Come again, Azreen was a guy?! Man, this was güüd.

The gist of it was, there was an apartment somewhere in Brickfields. Serene Mansions. Any member of the group could use it, by posting their intention on the chat, on a first-come first-served basis.

Occupancy was brisk. Even more so since the lifting of the MCO. Irfan himself had been checking in a few times a week.

Then had come the cryptic requests for money, veiled in, 'Aah haa, titayo, I know, aiyoyo' type messages from unknown mobile nos.

The amounts were not large, a couple of hundred ringgit each time. Irfan had always coughed up and naively hoped that was it.

Of course, his wife knew nothing of his main kayu tiga, which, aptly in Irfan's case, translated into English as 'playing three woods'.

Would she have really minded, though? Romy suddenly realized he'd never heard Kak Shila express an opinion nor say a word which contradicted her husband's. She was submissive to that degree.

Unlike his ex-wife. He couldn't even say tomaytoes, without her screeching, "Tomahtoes, Romy, to-mah-toes!"

Then, just that afternoon, the murder had happened.

Scared shitless, Irfan had fled the scene.

Almost immediately afterward, there was a message.

But the request had ballooned to fifty thousand ringgit. This time, accompanied by several photos, including one of a shocked Irfan bending over the body of his dead lover, captured by a CCTV camera.

Irfan, in true Malaysian fashion, had pleaded for a discount.

The reply had been, pay 30k first and the remainder within three days, plus another 10k in a week, as penalty for late payment.

After several unsuccessful attempts at haggling, which had taken the best part of an evening, he transferred the first 30 grand before calling Romy.

"It's not so much the money, even though it is a lot," Irfan was saying. "But Shila must never find out. She'll be so angry and hurt."

Romy rolled his eyes. Didn't his brother geddit? He had a homicide charge on his back and a blackmailer on his tail. Yet, he was scareder of upsetting his wife.

"You don't know the real Kak Shila, 'My," Irfan went on soberly. "She's a lioness at home."

A disturbing image of his sister-in-law in a Nala outfit flitted through Romy's mind, which he immediately quashed.

"And now Azreen is dead and it's been made to look like I killed him. If it comes out, how will Shila cope with the scandal? Family honor means everything to her." Irfan was practically bawling. Like a girl.

Romy was about to retort, *Kak Shila will just have to swallow her pride.*

Then his heart melted when he remembered the children.

He was fond of his nephews and niece, especially the second boy, Asyraf. Nice kids, all grown now. The youngest and smartest had just had her graduation ceremony online, which was so unfair. *Damn Covid.*

"I have a spare phone. You tell the blackmailer to contact that number, 'Bang. I'll deal with the bastard."

"Yeah, but the murder? What if the police do have something more than the photos, that they can pin on me?"

"'Kay, just tell me exactly what happened. Slow-w-w-ly, 'Bang, take your time. And don't bullshit me." May as well rub it in. This time, there was no mistaking the glee in his voice. "No wurries, Big Bro, I won't breathe a word to Mak."

×

It was the morning after the murder of the afternoon before.

PI Romy took a large gulp of his Malta in its cold glass and breathed a sigh of satisfaction.

From his vantage point on the terrace, he surveyed the immaculately mowed fairways and greens of the country's most prestigious Golf Club.

"Lemme meet your TBTM pals after your game," Romy had suggested to Irfan. "I mean, you have to carry on like normal. And who knows, I might be able to prove something to help your case."

Normally, his brother would've been unenthusiastic. Because Romy was a bit of a jakun in high-class company. And the only thing he might prove, would be just an Embarrassment with a capital E.

But Irfan was desperate. "Orait, 'My. But for God's sake, don't act like you own the place."

Sure. Like telling Datin Vivy she must never vlog about her have-have life.

Romy basked in his present ambience of atas-ness, like a mat rempit who'd inadvertently wandered into a Ducati showroom. This was the life, man.

Snapping his fingers at the waiter for more ice, he casually removed his premium fake Ray-Ban Wayfarers and chucked them on the table. Like. A. Boss.

In the distance, he could make out Irfan with his buddies on the last green.

He thought through again, his brother's version of events.

A sensational murder such as this was bound to have been in the news.

Especially when the caddy was an employee at such a prestigious club, which counted royalty and politicians amongst its members.

But there had been no reports.

And nothing on the News.

Something didn't add up.

Romy had also made cautious enquiries from his sources, including a reliable one at the HKL mortuary.

He'd even messaged his clerk to do a second and third quick sweep of the internet's alternative news sites.

But all yielded yilek, as well.

Speaking of his clerk, she seemed to have misplaced her whoopee these last few days. Odd. Romy put it down to pre-wedding nerves. If he wasn't mistaken, the big day was three weeks away.

Back to the fateful previous afternoon.

Irfan had booked the apartment from 4pm till 6pm.

He'd arrived slightly late. A work email had popped up just as he was about to set off, which he attended to promptly, even though it could've waited till the Monday. Irfan was conscientious laidat.

He'd let himself in with the security passcode. To his surprise, the blinds were down and the place was in semi-darkness. Normally, Azreen was always there first, ready with a cup of Tongkat Ali tea.

"Tongkat Ali tea?" repeated Romy.

"You know I don't drink, 'My," Irfan said virtuously, catching sight of a telltale green and black six-pack on his Adik's kitchen counter. "Berdosa, tau."

God, Abang is such a pot, thought Romy.

Irfan had stumbled to the window to pull up the blinds, then almost passed out at the gory spectacle which met his eyes.

Azreen was sprawled face up on the queen-size bed, his head covered in blood. There was blood on the shaggy pile carpet below, too. A bloodstained golf stick, obviously the weapon, had been left next to him.

"Are you sure there was no one else still in there?" asked Romy.

Irfan was doubtful. "It's a studio apartment. Nowhere to hide. Unless he was behind the shower curtain."

"Or she. Or they." Romy had recently taken to making a show of being politically correct when he could. A new habit he'd picked up, after being an adventitious spare wheel at a girly lunch of A-list besties.

Irfan had left the place in a panic. But he'd had the cow sense before then to wipe his prints off the blinds, front door handle and entry keypad.

Romy frowned as he gazed yet again at the photos his brother had forwarded to him. That golf stick in the first photo – it was at a different angle from the one in the third photo.

The whole sordid episode seemed too bizarre to be real. Like it had all never actually happened. Because the cleaners would've come in at around 7 pm, to do the housekeeping in time for the next booking at 9 pm, they would definitely have screamed blue murder all the way round the corner to the nearest police station.

9 pm had also come and long gone. Not a squeak.

Then, this morning too, the feathered foursome had faithfully turned up for their usual game, as punctual as shopaholics at a Black Friday sale.

There was something about the whole situation Romy couldn't quite put his finger on. Some sort of fowl play, he wouldn't be surprised.

His thoughts were broken by an irritatingly familiar voice calling, "'My!"

Four sweaty golfers plonked themselves round the table.

"Hi there," a short stocky man in a signature Lacoste polo shirt greeted him genially. "I'm Aznan Albari."

"PI Romy. Honored to meet you, Tan Sri," murmured Romy obsequiously, while attempting to exude a debonair charm beside such a modest billionaire.

"Just call me Barry," Tan Sri grinned widely, then winced slightly. He shifted in his seat to remove the cause of his discomfiture, which was his wallet in his back pocket.

"Hmm… Romy izzit? I'm Dato' Seri Ganesan," proffered a lofty-looking gentleman, kitted out to the nines in Calvin Klein. "Sunny to my close friends," he added pleasantly, with an emphasis on the word *close*.

"Yes, Dato' Seri, of cause," Romy tended to muddle his homonyms when his betters put him in his place.

Irfan was gesturing politely, "'My, you know Datuk Raffee."

Actually, he didn't. Neither had he ever heard of the person.

"The cosmetics king," added Irfan encouragingly.

"Eleven million lipsticks sold, you!" His Majesty had no reservations about tooting his own horn.

"Waah, then your name must be on everyone's lips!" Romy responded in awe, recovering some of his composure.

"That's lip service for you!" piped in the coy billionaire.

Datuk Raffee puckered his mouth in a not-unattractive pout. "But alas, when it comes to golf, my lips are sealed. So koyak, lah, my game today!"

"Ya, Datuk, I noticed," commented Irfan lightly. "Usually you use your Cobra F9 for that killer fourth hole. But it looks like you forgot to bring it."

"Hmm, maybe. How 'bout you, 'Fan," the Datuk shot back. "Where's your B21? You always swear by it for your long drives."

What's with this sudden switch to badass fighter aircraft, thought Romy, puzzled.

But Irfan replied glibly, "Oh, you mean my Big Bertha? The maid was meant to put it back in my bag after she cleaned it. But you know, kan, Datuk, these Indon maids…"

"I never let any of my domestic helpers touch my clubs," interjected Dato' Seri Ganesan – Sunny to his close friends – fussily. "Can't be trusted."

"Same here," chipped in Barry, the shy billionaire. "Can you imagine, I caught my houseboy using my Hoya crystal putter as a galah to pluck mangoes!"

"Haiyaa, really?" tutted Romy, sympathetically.

Heck, they were beginning to sound like a bevy of tai tai discussing their servants' foibles after a mahjong session.

"It's the same with caddies," Romy went on eagerly, in an attempt to be part of the flock. "Always taking liberties, I've heard. Worst is when you're just about to hit the ball and they decide to come from behind."

One could have knocked Irfan down with a feather, on hearing his Adik's graphic description. To his relief, the waiter created a diversion by appearing with their drinks.

Raffee pretended to make a grab for his pink jambu lemonade at the same time as the waiter was setting down the glass. Some of it spilled on the latter's immaculate white uniform.

"Careless little cock," the cosmetics king denounced archly, tapping the flustered servitor on the butt. His hand lingered on the latter's thigh, "Wouldn't you agree, sunny boy?"

It was obvious he was having a little dig at his close friend.

But Dato' Seri appeared not to have heard. Swishing his John Daly with a silver-tipped spoon, he proceeded to address Romy in a jocular fashion.

"So Romy, what sort of cases do you handle? Commercial espionage? Renegade employees? Cheating husbands?"

"Asking *fore* a friend, Dato' Seri?" quipped Irfan, in an effort to lighten the atmosphere.

Hah, so my uppity brother isn't on the close friends list either, Romy smirked to himself. Aloud, he replied pointedly, "Mostly murder, Dato' Seri."

There was a sharp intake of breath from the others.

Barry's initial guffaw at Irfan's wit faded away to a hiccup, while holding his half-drunk Arnold Palmer in mid air.

Datuk Raffee's coquettish smile, which had been playing on his lips, died instantly.

A cloud suddenly appeared over Sunny's previously clement countenance.

Irfan stroked his chin in a nervous gesture.

You could cut the air with a knife, thought Romy irrelevantly.

Eventually, Datuk Raffee spoke. "Put your glass down lah, Barry."

The demure billionaire shot him a quizzical look and remarked lightly, as he slowly laid it down, "The longer I hold it up, the heavier it becomes. Same as the worries in life. The more one worries, the greater the stress."

Okay, thought Romy, *so now we've moved on to life coaching tips.*

"Yup, like sitting in a rocking chair. All that motion but you don't get anywhere," he chipped in, proud to be able to add to the conversation in a productive way.

Nobody seemed to know how to respond to that.

Raffee merely giggled as he scooped the fleshy bits of jambu from his lemonade. Some of the liquid squirted onto Irfan's embroidered Givenchy polo shirt.

Romy could see Irfan struggling to be a sport about it.

Barry gulped down the rest of his drink and winked broadly. "Gotta go."

"See ya, Barry," called out Romy breezily. It wasn't often he was on matey terms with a billionaire and he was danged if he didn't want the whole club to know about it.

Raffee glanced fussily at his Audemars Piguet timepiece.

Exclaiming loudly, "Oh my! I'm late, I'm late! For my most intriguing date!" He skipped off nimbly before anyone could comment.

Sunny (but only to his nearest and dearest, if you don't mind) stood Irfan and Romy another round of drinks.

A bit sombong but not such a bad chap, opined Romy, slurping the froth off the rim of his Bell's Robust.

Irfan, predictably, sipped daintily at his Tongkat Ali soda.

Sunny swigged another JD, as he read his phone messages and appeared deep in reflection on a private dilemma of his own.

Romy's phone pinged suddenly. He took it out of his right trouser pocket to check, then realized it was his other number in the left pocket. The one he'd instructed Irfan to tell the blackmailer to contact.

"Just need ta sprinkle ma tinkle," he murmured grandly, and meandered off in the direction of the Men's.

The message was just two words. 'Serene 3pm'.

Automatically, Romy thumbed in, 'k'.

$$\times$$

It was 2 pm.

The double pint of Bell's had sufficed in lieu of lunch. Romy was going out to tea later but now he was feeling kinda peckish.

Not to mention, he was beginning to get cold feet about this unexpected summons at 3 pm. After all, the next 20 grand wasn't due for a couple more days.

Romy hadn't mentioned the message to Irfan.

When his Abang had asked, just before they parted ways at the club carpark at noon, "Any updates?" Romy replied airily, "Kautim, Bro."

Pressed further by Irfan's "How, 'My?", Romy had merely mumbled cryptically, as he carelessly, carefully clicked his Bezza remote (*some day it'll be my Porsche Macan, uolls*), "I got my cable."

Why worry his Abang needlessly. *I'll work something out*, thought Romy, ever the optimist.

He scrabbled about in his fridge and found a solitary pisang goreng.

Chewing it ruminatively, he recalled it was from his favorite teatime stall on Jalan Thambipillay. Of course this piece didn't taste so great anymore, being fridging cold for one.

He stared at the photos on his phone again. Nothing.

Romy abstractedly reached for another bite of pisang goreng to discover the bag was empty. Then he remembered. Wasn't Serene Mansions a stone's throw away from the pisang goreng stall?

'Killing two birds with one stone' would be how his bossy ex-wife would put it.

Romy didn't like that phrase. There was something heartless about it.

The Malay equivalent was 'Sambil menyelam minum air'. Which didn't sound particularly enjoyable either. Except, maybe, if it was something other than seawater. *And no, not Seamaster. Something with more oomph.. Jägermeister, maybe, huhuhu.*

He fished up his Bezza keys from its hook by the front door.

$$\times$$

The guard at the lobby of Serene Mansions was too absorbed swiping sweets on his Samsung to even glance up as Romy, replete with five freshly fried pisang goreng inside him, made his way swiftly into the conveniently open lift.

A chap like myself in this new normal of face masks, can pass for anyone, ranging from Remy Ishak to Radhi Khalid, mused Romy, fancifully.

Sporting a pair of plastic gloves was perfectly acceptable too. The Covid situation with its protocols had its pluses.

Luck was on his side. The security entry code into the apartment hadn't been changed. The discreet CCTV camera, surprisingly, was off.

The whole place sparkled and shone like a new pin. Not a speck. Marie Kondo would've been proud.

Romy patted the neon green sateen bedsheet. *Oh, but they'd missed a spot.* There was a single long stray hair on the pillow. Romy snapped a photo, then kept away the hair in a small ziplock bag he always brought when he went detecting.

He pulled back the sheet to check the mattress. The quilted Jean Perry protector was clean, without any hint of stains, blood or otherwise. He knew there had to be some detail he'd missed, some fact which had escaped his attention.

Still nothing.

Then he caught sight of something just barely visible under the bed. A wallet. He'd seen one just like it not long ago.

Irrelevantly, he suddenly remembered: *Crap!* He was meant to be picking up his ex-wife and Aiman to take them to tea at his mother's.

It was a monthly ritual, initiated by Mak herself after his divorce. To prove she bore no rancor toward her son's ex-wife, thereby dispelling the trope of the evil mother-in-law in a P. Ramlee movie.

He would never hear the end of it if he were late.

Instinctively pocketing the wallet in the same ziplock bag, he slipped noiselessly out of the apartment. He heard the lift doors opening, accompanied by voices.

More discreet to take the stairs.

It was nineteen floors down but no sweat. Romy was fit like that.

He pushed open the fire door and was about to sprint down when – *holy excrement!*

Slumped on the staircase landing, eyes wide shut, cherry red lips pouted in agony, was a very dead Datuk Raffee. Still in his RLX Polo shirt and chinos of that morning.

He'd obviously suffered several blows to the head. Not to mention a gaping wound from a knife stuck dramatically into his chest.

Romy's heels sprouted wings. He was out of the building in three minutes. It was his personal best.

$$\times$$

His ex-wife, dressed in her 'new arrival' Zara high neck poplin top and pleated palazzo pants, sat primly with her seatbelt slung over a large cardboard package balanced on her lap.

She was carefully made-up, as usual.

"You look quite nice," Romy said, trying to make amends for having kept her and Aiman waiting for fifteen minutes.

"It must be my new lipstick."

"Eleven million sold, you," murmured Romy.

"How d'you know?" His ex-wife was momentarily impressed. Then, "Don't change lanes so abruptly just like that. Signal first. You can see I'm holding a cake."

"Backseat driver," muttered Romy crossly.

But it sounded like bake instead of back, which got his ex-wife chortling, "Bake seat driver, ha ha, 'My."

"So my England not as powderful as yours. Baa-ack, baa-ck!" he retorted.

God, she always got his goat. And he'd wanted things pleasant between them for a change, with his special edition Perodua Bezza Advance and premium fake Wayfarers. Not to mention her new Zara outfit, eleven million lipsticks and all.

"Baa-ack," he added once more.

"You're acting like a kid, Pa," said Aiman, rolling his eyes.

Romy stuck out his lower lip and looked mutinous.

Inwardly though, he was shitting bricks.

He'd seen his fair share of stiffs dumped in back alleys and stairwells in his line of work. Not to mention the devastation in Mogadishu and Sarajevo during his time in the army.

But this was totes out of his league.

The whole charade of teatime small talk between Mak and his ex-wife, punctuated by Aiman's running commentary on the latest Chelsea premier league match, grated on his nerves, big time.

Even the cake his ex-wife had brought, annoyed him. It wasn't her usual Banoffee chocolate cake, which he liked, but some fancy concoction with tea leaves in it.

"It's all over Instagram, Romy. Everyone's raving about Earl Grey butter cream cakes."

Ya, so?

His ex-wife was bleating, "Mak, I simply cannot decide. Should I get the Marc Jacobs tote bag that's on sale?"

"If you ask my view, anything Gucci is always better value," his mother replied. "Especially kalau the design ada the Gucci monogram."

"Yes, that's true. If only Gucci weren't so expensive," sighed his ex-wife wistfully.

Enough was enough.

Romy barked at his ex-wife, "All this mindless chatter giving me a headache. You and Aiman take Grab back. I'm very busy, got important things to do."

Besides, who was this Marc Jacobs dude anyway. He sounded like some state hockey player from Kampung Portugis.

Once he was in his car, Romy Googled his phone. Not for Marc. But for Raffee.

This time, the news portals were nearly on the verge of crashing. What got him scared shitless was the one-liner which kept cropping up:

An unidentified man was spotted driving away from the crime scene in a red Bezza.

He dropped his phone on the floorboard like a hot potato.

Eh, what was that in the ziplock bag, which he'd shoved down the side of his seat?

Fark. The wallet.

What the heck was he thinking, bolting out with crucial evidence like that. He was such a nutter sometimes and now, just short of being totally screwed.

Nice wallet, though. Top quality leather. A Bottega Veneta bifold. Very classy. Where had he seen one recently like it? He wouldn't mind having one for himself. His present Tommy Hilfiger from mudah.my was showing serious signs of wear and tear.

He opened it wide.

Ensconced within the clear polymer insert, was the MyKad of… hold on, not Raffee, the late cosmetics king… but Barry, the unassuming billionaire.

Daaamn, WTF.

The ping of his phone startled him out of his transient reverie.

He slipped his hand in his pocket. Again, it was his other phone.

'*$$ cyberjaya come now'.

Obediently Romy thumbed in his usual 'k'.

✕

Upgrading works on the MEX meant it took longer for Romy to get to Cyberjaya.

He decided to park a street away from the venue. Best to be discreet.

He worried a little, though, about someone taking a fancy to his Bezza's sports rims. Or even just running a coin along the side of the car door. *Because, well, you know lah, people are known to be inexplicably jealous laidat.*

He entered the café after going through the usual charade of checking in on his MySejahtera, then hearing his temperature recited by a disembodied Japanese voice.

It was fairly crowded.

But Romy was able to find a low table with comfortable leather chairs, which gave off an ambience of being in a gentlemen's club, sort of.

He took a cautious swig of his double shot shaken espresso and waited.

The two people who slid quietly into the chairs opposite, with their caramel macchiatos, had masks on.

As Romy had mused earlier, these Covid protocols had their pluses.

In the dimly-lit café, the fellow could've passed for anyone ranging from Shah Rukh Khan to Indi Nadarajah. But Romy knew damn well who he was. They'd been having drinks together just that morning.

The other was a woman. *Ah, hence the stray souvenir on the pillow.* He knew they'd also met before but he couldn't quite place her. Again, with her mask on, she could be anyone from Jennifer Lopez to Nur Fazura.

Romy was livid. It was lucky the place was noisy because he practically yelled across the table. "Why involve my brother in your sick parlor games?"

It was Dato' Seri Ganesan who spoke first.

"I didn't. It was Raffee. His idea of a joke. I knew he was sadistic. Easily jealous. He couldn't take it when that Azreen boy favored Irfan. But we didn't think it would end up in murder and blackmail."

Romy remarked in a daze, "Raffee killed Azreen and pinned it on my brother?" He looked at the Dato' Seri. "And then you killed Raffee?"

Dato' Seri shook his head.

"No, I killed him," said the second person, speaking for the first time.

Romy thought immediately, *I know that voice.*

It was Datin Harlina.

"With Barry's help," she added coolly.

Ah yes, Barry, the bashful billionaire.

"Why?" Romy genuinely wanted to know.

"Because Raffee was an arsehole and a bully," replied the Datin, matter-of-factly. "He was also screwing my late husband. And Barry's soon-to-be ex-wife. I gave Barry the heads up on his wife and Raffee. Raffee swings both ways, so it was easy for me to arrange a hookup with him at the apartment. When he saw Barry, he thought we'd be a jolly threesome. Well, it was jolly for Barry and me but not so much for Raffee, as you saw. We thought it best to tuck him away on the stairs, rather than cluttering the apartment. Despite that, it was quite a job putting everything in apple-pie order again."

Hmm, your maid skills must've come in useful, thought Romy, curling his lip superciliously.

She went on. "I nicked Barry's wallet and left it for you to find, after I took some photos. Then I put it in an anonymous call to alert the police about the murder."

"Why try to implicate Barry?" Romy was puzzled.

"Because now he'll have to marry me. It won't do Barry any favors if I share photos on Twitter, of his wallet beside Raffee's body. So," she held out an elegant Cartier beringed hand. "PI Romy, the wallet, please."

Romy slowly handed her the wallet.

Dato' Seri Ganesan saw his reluctance. It was, after all, a really nice wallet.

"Romy, I can buy one for you," he said. He wasn't a bad chap.

Romy thought for a moment. Then he said, "If you don't mind, Dato' Seri, can you make it a Gucci monogram purse instead? For my ex-wife," he added humbly. "I couldn't buy her expensive things, you see. That's why she left me."

4

✕

PI ROMY LETS THE CAT OUT OF THE BAG

✕

PI Romy was reading the newspapers.

What a depressing start to the new year.

Another deadly strain of the Covid virus had been detected at a construction site…

Abah was due to announce yet another lockdown and was also planning to suspend Parliament…

Suicide rates were increasing threefold…

Hospitals were near breaking point, with medical workers suffering from burnout…

Sheesh. It was the same old, same old.

Damn Covid.

It was also driving people to do untypical things. Like stealing truckloads of milk formula and baby diapers.

But apparently the authorities finally had a lead on the latest in a series of such hijackings at the gudang pejabat Kastam in Pengkalan Hulu by a group dubbed the Infantry gang.

Pengkalan Hulu? All these name changes. Ah yes, Kroh. That was its original name. Somewhere in the northern part of Perak, near the Thai border.

As a newly minted Army rat, Romy had been stationed in Kroh for a few months. Within what had been known as a 'black area' during the Communist insurgency in the '60s to '80s, but that was before his time.

His training stint at Kroh had been rigorous, to put it mildly. There were tactical exercises in the dense and unforgiving jungle. Strangely enough, it was the extended Z wall traverse, on the assault course just behind their base, which was the killer. None of his platoon, except for an hombre called Dahlan from Long Sukang in the northern region of Sarawak, ever completed it without blubbering like a baby.

But just a bus ride across the border from Kroh was Betong town, with arguably the raunchiest after-hours entertainment on offer south of Bangkok.

He recalled a hilariously louche pre-dawn expedition with his dorm mates, Hafiz and Yi Tong to a –

His phone buzzed.

Romy glanced at the message on the screen. *Damnit, was the bloke telepathic* – because it was Yi Tong.

The message read, 'Japanese at Pavi?'

Ya, why not. Last kopek, before KL entered its second lockdown. *That bloody Covid.*

The Pavilion shopping center was unfamiliar territory to Romy. And sushi was what he termed a bit too makanan anak lord for his plebeian palate.

But as his mate was paying… Romy wasn't the type who checked the price tag before accepting a gift.

Yi Tong, or Philip, as he now preferred to be called since his discharge from the army, was already at the restaurant.

Yowzer, he'd brought along a girl.

Okay, not quite a girl. But her slim figure and elfin features belied her age. Hands don't lie. The right side of 40, Romy's guess was correct.

There was something gamine about her beauty. Like that classic actress his ex-wife admired. Audrey someone or other. But there was a hunted expression in her dark hazel eyes, which reminded Romy of a gazelle. No, more enigmatic. A panther, or maybe a clouded leopard. Or some other equally exotic cat.

"My cousin, Rachel," said Philip.

Romy took in the Dior monogram of her odd shaped bag, tucked snugly under a well-toned arm. Her plain white shirt discreetly spelled Armani while her strategically ripped Levi's 501 skinnies showed off her legs to their best advantage.

"She got a problem," Philip went on.

Ah, the prospect of business. Good, good. Romy grinned at her widely, in what he hoped was a reassuring manner.

At Philip's suggestion, he decided on a katsukarē. It sounded far more exotic than what it was: fried chicken cutlets in a curry sauce over a bowl of rice.

Philip had the same.

Rachel nibbled on a seaweed wrap, which to Romy's astonishment was called a California roll.

"But then, I guess we have our roti John and sup gearbox," he mused, with a hearty chuckle.

Rachel smiled weakly back.

Romy saw that she was actually close to tears. "Okeh Miss Rachel, how you want me to help you?" he asked sympathetically, while in his mind, confidently categorizing her problem under 'cheating boyfriend'.

"PI Romy, I need you protect my litter boy, Cooper. He's in a lot of danger, one."

Romy was taken aback. Kids were not within his job scope. "Er… shouldn't you go to the police?"

"It's what I kept telling her," agreed Philip, pouring more iced green tea into their glasses.

A pair of crystal teardrops rolled down from her Charlotte Tilbury mascara-lined eyes onto her Fenty Beauty-contoured cheeks. She had missed a layer though, so one cheekbone was infinitesimally lighter than the other. "No. No police, one."

Romy caught snatches of her murmured aside to her cousin.

"Tung king… kwan hai. Ngor chee hai… 'Hidden paw yat sei sei' yau. Moo yan ho yee chap sau…"

Romy balked. "Ho sui lor… you're talking kongsi gelap? Ya, I also dowan play-play with them."

"Ehh, you speak Cantonese, meh?" exclaimed Rachel.

"PI Romy went to Chinese school, maa," said Philip.

"Only till Primary five," murmured Romy modestly.

"You don't worry about your charges, PI Romy," she assured him, her voice rising a few decibels. "I got money. I can pay one."

"Oh, it's not about that, Miss Rachel," Romy struggled between gallantry and prudence. Against his better judgment, he threw the latter to the winds. "Why don't you tell me more about it?" he asked gently.

Rachel shook her head vehemently. "No, cannot. You just have to promise me you'll take care of my boy. Dat's all. I pay you, you don't worry, one. I know you are kind man, PI Romy," she wheedled. "Philip got tell me one time when he come back, some of de bad, bad tings happen when you was both of you in dat war place. An' how you hep so much de peepels."

Romy was silent. It was one of the episodes in his army career he always tried to forget.

Philip started checking his phone for messages which weren't there. He didn't want to be reminded, either.

Acutely aware that she had touched a raw nerve, Rachel fiddled with her Phoebe from *Friends*-inspired locket, then took out a pen and doodled on her napkin.

A sudden beep on her iPhone 11 startled her. "I have to go. So long oredi I leave Cooper by hisself at home."

Romy was quite horrified. "What, there's no one to jaga your son while you go out?"

"Is not hiss first time, PI Romy," Rachel replied nonchalantly, folding her paper napkin into a tinier and tinier square. "My boy, he very clever, one."

"How old did you say he is?" asked Romy weakly.

"I never say one. He tree years old but so smart, weyy. So you promise me, PI Romy?" Her voice was getting whingey.

Akin to his ex-wife's pleading tone when there had been a trinket she wanted from Pandora, which he could ill afford. But just the tone was similar. Rachel's England was nowhere close to his ex-wife's league.

"You take care my boy? PI Romy, pliss, pliss. I pay you, you no worry, one. So, can?"

"Uh, well, I – I – okeh, can." Romy felt almost compelled to raise his hands where she could see them.

But Rachel wasn't going to let the matter rest there. "You promise? Swear to God you take care my boy?"

Romy hesitated.

"PI Romy. You swear to God?"

There was a desperation bordering on psychosis, in her eyes.

"Er… erm… uhh… ya…"

"Thank you, PI Romy," Rachel took his mammering as an affirmative. "And God bless you. I'll be in touch."

There was no doubting the gratitude and relief in her voice.

Rapidly donning her Tory Burch mask, she said to her cousin, "Ah Phil, ah. Here, take my condo key card, in case anyting. Oh ya, I visit your Ma yesterday. I tink she oredi nyanyuk, lah. She keep call me Nicole."

With a flash of a comely, bare knee through an exceptionally wide tear in her jeans, she unfurled her legs from beneath her chair.

In a single glide of her Nike Air Force Ones, she vanished out of the restaurant.

"Who's Nicole?" asked Romy curiously.

"Her twin. Actually, they both had it tough. Their parents died, train accident, when they were kids."

"Oh ya? That's very sad."

"None of the relatives wanted them because they were regarded as suei," Philip's tone was matter-of-fact. "So Po Po sent them to live at the temple. My Ma was the only one who cared a bit, brought them to our house, sometimes." He reminisced, "She would follow me round like a puppy."

"Huh? Your Mother?" exclaimed Romy in surprise.

"No lah, you goon. Rachel. Nicole was the quiet one, always kept to herself."

"You mention they're twins. Must be identical, that's why your Ma mistook one for the other."

"They both look only, same-same. Rachel got not much upstairs but clever to make money. Used to be a famous catwalk model. Nicole very smart but siao. Studied in London. So speaks like the Queen but works for lousy pay with one of those NGOs."

"Hmm," said Romy absently, losing interest.

"How 'bout some daifuku?" suggested Philip. "It's a dessert," he added hastily.

Romy declined. "Thanks for the lunch, Bro."

It had been good to touch base with his old army buddy. They went back a long way.

Trudging warily and wearily in a tour of duty during an exceptionally bleak Balkan winter, they had promised each other that if one of them didn't make it, the one who did would visit the other's mother.

He walked rapidly in the direction of the carpark.

More unwanted memories surfaced. That little Bosnian boy barely out of nappies... *Hamad? – Yousef? – Sohayb? – no, Emir. Emir Mehmedinović.* Hiding for a week in the rubble of that carpet-bombed neighborhood in Sarajevo.

It was pure chance that Romy and Yi Tong, as he then was, had stumbled upon the little nipper.

With an effort, he blanked out the tragic event that followed.

He was about to get into his Bezza when a coquettish voice hailed him from the driver's window of a low slung sports car.

"PI Romy! What a lovely surprise!"

Romy preened slightly at the compliment, while wishing he could recall whose voice it was behind the Alia Bastamam mask and Loewe eyeglasses.

"Oh, you've forgotten me," went on the voice, in mock disappointment.

A slender figure slid gracefully out of the car toward him.

"Tengku Amaryllis," he remembered just in time.

He regretted hurrying down to the carpark. It would've been more prestigious if they'd bumped into each other in a crowd. Then again, where was there ever a crowd these days... unless at a durian party hosted by a YB.

She was holding her trademark miniscule Fendi bag in one elegant hand.

On the wrist of her other hand, she carried a capacious handbag. Romy thought it was one of the ugliest bags he had ever seen. His ex-wife, though, would've been awestruck. But then, Romy couldn't be expected to know it was a Birkin 35 Vert Maquis.

He was even more nonplussed to hear little snuffling sounds coming from within.

"My baby," the Tengku whispered proudly.

"Oh ya?" To his recollection, she had only been married a month or two.

"We decided to adopt," she added blithely. "Doing our small part to save the world, one baby at a time."

"Oh ya," repeated Romy, for want of anything else to say.

"Would you like to hold him?"

Before he could reply, a furry ball was thrust into his unsuspecting arms.

It was all he could do, not to scream like a girl. "Oh, a cat," he remarked weakly. He hated cats, so geli. "Is he for real?"

Tengku Amaryllis roared with laughter. "Fur real! As real as my Fur-rari here," she exclaimed, patting the gleaming white bonnet of her car. "How pawfully witty. PI Romy, you are sooo a-mewsing!"

Her Jimmy Choo kitten heels tapped the ground skittishly as she walked toward the escalator, still chortling.

Have-have people are confirm weird, Romy mused, as he maneuvered his Bezza round the carpark onto Jalan Bukit Bintang.

That Rachel, though. She seemed so desperate. At the same time, there was something – unreal? try hard? – about her.

And how could anyone's English be so appalling. Conversing with her, Romy had felt almost like Henry Higgins.

Of course, it had only been when Romy was courting his ex-wife that he'd ever watched a musical. Surprisingly, he'd enjoyed it.

Another thing, how did Philip come to tell her about Emir? The subject was taboo.

Then again, Romy had spent two decades in the army, several in active service. There were a lot of subjects which were taboo.

War. He could never see the point of it.

A lot of yapping amongst the superpowers and superficial outpourings of sympathy from those safely far away from it all.

Meanwhile, the devastation and slaughter carried on like – what was the phrase used by that character in the film he watched recently on Astro Boo? *Ah yes,* "'cam selamba aje."

Yet, within the shrapnel-riddled walls of a tiny church, amidst the bloodied corpses of the congregation, some with their hands clasped in a final gesture of prayer, Yi Tong the agnostic had found humanity's salvation in Christ.

Romy, on the other hand, caned into submission by his Ustaz at eight years old for daring to query God's will as to why his Abang could pass his exams while he couldn't, when he'd also studied, suddenly found his hitherto unshakable imaan wavering.

Fortunately, Mak put a stop to that. "Kamu kahwin je, 'My. You're nearly forty. Pergi cari a nice girl. Kan, ikut sunnah, when a man has married, he has completed one half of his religion."

Romy had suggested similarly to Philip when the latter confessed he often still awoke to the sound of shell fire ringing in his ears. "For the companionship." But Philip stayed resolutely single and was content most of the time not to mingle.

Romy's free lunch had made him sluggish.

Luckily, he always kept a sports kit handy in his car. Instead of continuing straight, he decided to turn right at the traffic lights. Perhaps he'd sneak a run round Sentul Park.

He was pally with the security head there. The guy was a distant relative and Romy had also helped him out on a delicate matter once. Some unpleasantness with one of the cleaning ladies, who'd mistakenly thought his relative's intentions were noble, *huhuhu.*

Nothing like a workout in the afternoon heat to test his stamina.

He parked discreetly near The Maple.

But damn, he was sleepy. All that Japanese curry.

An Egyptian PT instead would be nice, especially as the front seat had a decent recline.

Nope, he told himself firmly. *A man's gotta do what a man's gotta do.*

But the next thing he knew, the azan for Asar prayers was sounding from a neighborhood surau.

Shit, he'd slept for an hour.

Still time enough for his run, though. Looking round to see that it was safe to do a Superman in his Bezza, he saw a few figures in the distance.

Their faces were turned away, which was good.

Thirty seconds was plenty for him to swap his Padinis and Timberlands for his Under Armour and Asics.

With a dozen hamstring sweeps and twenty burpees as a warmup, the five rounds along the edge of the lake was a breeze.

Good things come to those who sweat. His mehness cleared completely.

Now for a cold shower at home.

As he drove slowly past the KLPAC carpark (heck, all those theater groups must be having it especially tough), a shoe suddenly fell out of the vehicle ahead.

Urgh, some people, tutted Romy to himself in disgust. Wasn't this meant to be a classy neighborhood?

He made a mental note of the number plate.

✕

The next few days came and went without incident and little activity.

The only topic of mild interest in the news was that there was an inexplicable shortage of vaccines in the country. Someone had been quietly buying and hoarding them.

Not the Covid vaccine, which seemed to be taking the scenic route to reach the nation's shores. But the vaccines they routinely gave to babies, to prevent infections like TB, polio and other virulent childhood diseases.

There was still no word from Rachel.

Her words, "I pay you. You don't worry, one," rang wistfully in Romy's ears.

Not that he was tapped out but with what looked like no end to this Covid shit, it was always handy to line his bank account.

Truth be told, he was also bored.

So bored he even tried engaging in small talk with his clerk.

Her wedding plans appeared to have been postponed indefinitely. Very casually, as if in passing, he attempted to risk asking her why. Her answers were monosyllabic.

Eventually, she remarked sardonically, "Why would I want a man? I already have a cat."

Too late, Romy realized she thought he was attempting to proposition her. He couldn't decide, between them both, who was the sadder.

He was about to head home early when his phone pinged with a message and a link for directions.

To his disappointment, it wasn't Rachel. *But ya! Philip also can, lah.*

Romy waltzed out of his office, and whistled as he went down the stairs.

✕

He didn't need to use Waze. He'd parked just beside it a few days ago when he'd sneaked into the area for his run.

Philip met him outside the entrance to the building.

"Rachel's one is on the 26th floor."

The whole apartment looked as though Lara Croft had woken up in it one morning and decided she hated everything.

The automated air freshener was partly effective in eliminating any odors likely to emanate in a closed area. But not effective enough, with the windows being shut and packets of half-opened food scattered in the kitchen.

"Someone was looking for something," Romy liked to state the obvious. "Any sign of her?"

Philip shook his head. "It was Nicole who asked me to pop by. They always text each other everyday and Nicole never heard from Rachel since last Sunday."

"Same day we met for makan," observed Romy sagely. Stating the obvious was proving to be the hallmark of Romy's sleuthing skills. His next question was slightly different. "Where's Nicole?"

"I donno. The last time, she told me she's based somewhere in Gerik."

"Nice place," remarked Romy.

"Gerik? Yeah. I remember we were stationed near there, those days."

"No, you mangkuk, I mean this condo. A lot of nice things."

"Yeah."

Indeed there were.

A large Straits Chinese Famille Rose bowl emblazoned with a dragon and peonies motif.

An exquisite Art Deco figurine of a dancer.

A pair of Wedgewood Jasperware candlesticks.

Meissen porcelain decorative plates.

Floral etched design Waterford crystal goblets.

An oversized vase which could pass for Ming.

Not that Romy was au faît in les beaux arts. But his Mak Ngah had been executive housekeeper at the Istana Di Raja of one of the previous Sultans, and often regaled her sister, Romy's mother, with pointers as to what was tasteful and what was tacky.

Miraculously, despite having been hurtled, tossed and flung about in the bid to look for that elusive something, none of the items were broken. Even the candlesticks, which had obviously fallen a substantial height from the sideboard onto the marble floor, were still intact.

Romy peered into the bedrooms. The second one had obviously been converted to a walk-in closet. Clothes, makeup, bags, shoes, were strewn all over the floor.

Again, fortuitously, there were no rips or tears to any of the clothes. Some of the makeup containers suffered slight dents but the bags had merely been swept off the shelves onto the carpet.

Romy could imagine his ex-wife's awed expression at the treasure trove of handbags. He could see a couple of LVs, a Chanel, several Guccis, Prada of course and other logos he couldn't recognize but they all looked fancy.

The collection of shoes was also impressive. Balenciaga. Ferragamo. YSL. Tod's. Even a pair of red lacquered stilettos, which reminded Romy of a movie he'd watched with his ex-wife years ago. From its title, he'd assumed it was a supernatural thriller but it proved to be nothing like. His ex-wife had been in thrall at the outfits of the three women in the movie, whereas Romy had been simply bored.

One of the shoes seemed out of place. A single Nike trainer. It looked like the partner of the one that had been flung out of the car window the other day. Inside it was a tiny, carefully folded tissue.

No, a paper napkin. The same one he'd seen Rachel doodling on at lunch. And she'd been wearing a pair of Nikes then, too.

Romy unfolded the napkin. Scrawled on it were some random letters of the alphabet, a series of twelve numbers and then another set of six numbers.

Romy frowned to himself and put the napkin in his pocket. He went back into the living room.

Philip had picked up a framed photograph of his twin cousins and was saying, "What do we do, now, 'My? Inform police or how?"

Romy looked over Philip's shoulder at the photo and asked, "Rachel and Nicole, were they kam cheng, ah?"

His friend furrowed his brow. "Aiyah, I donno. I lost touch with them for years. Until Rachel called me last week, ask if I know someone who can help her."

"Cooper!" Guiltily, Romy realized he'd totally forgotten about the lad.

"I think Rachel and Cooper were taken together," deduced Philip sensibly. "Let's wait for the kidnappers to contact us."

As if on cue, there was the sound of the front door opening. Romy's hand felt for the reassuring holster of his baby G.

"Wah, so messy!" the man exclaimed to his female companion.

"Ya, lor." She lowered her mask a second to reveal the face of an efficient-looking young woman, then quickly put it up again.

"Hi," she said to Romy, as he was standing nearest the door. "I'm Natalie and this is my colleague Oliver. We're from Fook Tan real estate agency. You're too late. We already secured a buyer for this property. Actually, we met Miss Nicole here a few weeks ago to close the deal. She gave us a key card so we can also arrange for the sale of the furniture and loose items."

"You mean, Rachel," corrected Philip. "Nicole is her twin. We're not property agents. I'm Philip, their cousin."

Natalie smiled embarrassedly. "We have a lot of clients. Their names can be so confusing."

"We're just popping by to take a quick look again, before making an inventory of the things," explained Oliver.

A warning look from Romy prevented Philip from blurting out, "Actually, Rachel's missing, you know!"

Romy enquired casually, "Who else was here when you came, that time?"

Natalie looked at Oliver for confirmation. "Miss – er – Rachel only, I think."

"Wait, there could've been a kid playing in the other room," volunteered Oliver. "I heard someone dragging a toy on the floor."

After watching them shut the front door noiselessly on their way out, Philip said eagerly, "So. What d'you think, 'My? Something funny going on, I'm sure."

"Yes, there is something yang tak kena," admitted Romy. "But what?"

His eyes lingered briefly on the pictures on the walls. Again, an indication of acquired good taste. A Chong Siew Ying monochrome landscape. A pair of Fauzin Mustafa botanical drawings. A set of deftly executed pen & ink calligraphy sketches of a cat in various poses.

His mind went back to that single Nike shoe, right in the middle of the room. It seemed to be calling out to him.

"We can ask the guard downstairs if he saw anything," suggested Philip. "Maybe Rachel getting into a car with someone."

"'Kay."

The guard at the lobby counter was cooperative but initially not so helpful. He thought he had seen her leave but couldn't remember. So many people going in and out of the building.

"In a car? Van?" Romy tried to jog the guard's memory.

"I forgot. Sorry lah."

Philip absentmindedly took out a ten ringgit note.

The guard's memory was miraculously restored. He slapped his forehead. "Ya, ya, in a car. Miss Rachel was with two person, Boss. Oh, and one of the residents find a shoe on the road, pass to me. It look like Miss Rachel shoe that she always wear. But I already throw away."

"A Nike sports shoe?" suggested Romy. "And the other two people she went with? They were the same man and woman, who came in here just a while ago, right? In a Kia Sportage VNY 3099M."

"Ehh, how you know?"

Romy ignored him and remarked conversationally to Philip. "Nicole also owns a unit here?"

"Nah. Where can she afford, maa?" Glancing at the clock on the wall behind the counter, he added abruptly, "I gotta run. Bible study class online. But here, 'My. Keep the key card. In case you want to check out the condo again."

Pressing his remote to open his car door as they walked out together, he said soberly, "It's true what Rachel commented. Ma oredi nyanyuk. Last few times I saw her, she mistook me for my late dad."

"Hmm." Romy's mind was preoccupied with other stuff Rachel had said.

The hidden paw gang.

Perhaps he should check them out.

$$\times$$

No such gangs surfaced on the internet chat forums. He tried his luck on the dark web but also drew a blank. Had it just been a tale on her part?

He thought a while, then keyed in Rachel's name and bandied it about. When he was about to despair, a PM came in.

The opening price was RM500. Romy's counter offer was RM75. Eventually, both parties settled on RM120.

Romy did the required online transfer and waited. And waited.

Shit, man, he wasn't only beginning to feel pissed but also pissed *on*; what the average Mat who'd been scammed of a Camel leather jacket on Carousell would say, "kena kencing". He'd already been left dangling for 40 minutes, damnit.

The scanned photos which were eventually sent to him, deffo were not what he was expecting.

A chill went down his spine.

One was a copy of a death certificate. The other was a recent insertion in the 'In Memoriam' column of a Chinese newspaper. There was a pause and then a third photo popped up. Slightly blurry but the driver of the battered old pickup truck laden with baby supplies, making a getaway from the gudang pejabat Kastam was unmistakable.

Romy wasn't the sharpest parang in the kitchen. But ya, the pieces were starting to fit together.

Then he remembered his son Aiman saying, "Pa, you should join LinkedIn. It's what all professional people have. That's how you stalk them."

Now was a good time to sign up. He went directly to Nicole's profile. His instincts were correct.

What worried him, where was Cooper? The kuchi rat was missing for nearly a week now. And he was far too young to fend for himself, despite his mother's confident, "My boy very independent one."

Not to mention her frenetic pleas. "You take care my boy?… You promise?… PI Romy, you swear to God?"

His phone ringing made him jump.

Damn, he'd be lunging out at shadows, next.

Oh. It was his mother.

She had a sudden hankering for a particular homemade sauce, which was only sold from a van on the forecourt of Hock Choon supermarket.

All the way in Ampang, for God's sake. It didn't matter that Romy might be busy with something else.

"You go now and buy, 'My. Sekarang jugak, understood? Mak teringin makan rojak."

"But we're in the middle of MCO 2.0, Mak –"

"MCO dua kali lima kepala hotak kau!" Mak's expletives were invariably in Malay and always summed up a situation perfectly. She was old school and articulate Like That.

$\times$

Romy was about to get into his Bezza with two bottles of 'sos buah viral Uolls' when a familiar voice hailed him.

"PI Romy, we must stop meeting like this," giggled Tengku Amaryllis. "People might talk."

Romy flicked his hair back and simpered. Heck, the Tengku's flirty manner was making him feel almost frisky.

"How's – er – the baby, Tengku?" he asked courteously.

"My li'l busyuk boy?" She peeked into the capacious Balenciaga x Hello Kitty tote bag on her arm. "Shhh, he's asleep. I'm just about to collect his painting from the frame maker. I wanted it specifically fitted in a Rococo style frame because it's a commissioned piece. By 'Dilah,'" she added casually.

"Oh, you mean the artist, Fadilah Karim," Romy was impressed. "She does interesting portraits."

Squeals of laughter emanated from the peppy Princess. "Paw-traits! PI Romy, mon 'chat'-rie, ooh là là, you're the cat's whiskers, when it comes to wit!"

Cat's whiskers. That faintly fetid odor in the apartment. Busyuk Boy.

Romy stood transfixed as he watched the Tengku's curvy behind, snugly encased in a pair of Citizens of Humanity high rise jeans, sashay up the ramp into Hock Choon.

Yess! He'd cracked it.

✕

"What? You're telling me Rachel died some time ago and it was Nicole we met the other day?" Philip's shocked tone reverberated through the sound waves to the extent that Romy had to hold his phone away from his ear.

"So Ma was right about her," Philip conceded, with the benefit of hindsight. "But I still donno how you figured it out."

Romy tried unsuccessfully not to sound smug. "The signs were there. For one thing, her England was too atrocious to be real. Even by Malaysian standards," he added patriotically. "And LinkedIn also helped."

He took Philip's silence at this comment for blur, which it was.

"Very useful in my line of work, LinkedIn," he said airily. "That NGO Nicole works for," he went on. "It's to save poor babies in those villages where there's no health care. With Covid, the donations they rely on to carry out their work, dried up. That's why those diaper and milk formula raids."

"So they formed their own Robin Hood gang," Philip said slowly.

"Then Rachel suddenly died, and left a lot of money, property even, but no will. Very leceh when that happens."

"Oh God, did Nicole –"

"No, lah, Nicole not so siau laidat to kill her own twin sister," interjected Romy hastily. "Rachel died of Covid. It happened quite swiftly and was unexpected. As with such cases, the burial had to be very quick. And also before her death, with all the self isolation and social distancing, people forget or not so rajin to keep in touch. Nicole decided to take a shortcut by pretending to be Rachel. Bank also will only know when you inform them of the death. Everything online, so everyday she just sapu her sister's bank account bit by bit and was in the process of selling whatever Rachel owned. To support the NGO."

He continued to explain patiently, "Natalie and Oliver were in on it, too, for the commission they earn. If the plan koyak, they can use the excuse they didn't know. There're so many people 'alive' who are actually dead, you know."

"Ya, like those phantom voters," agreed Philip.

"But recently, one of Rachel's old flames had put a memorial notice in the newspaper to mark her passing. And the police were also closing in on the gang. Nicole panicked, in case the bank might find out about her scam. Not to mention getting caught for the hijackings. She'd deffo go to jail, man. So she changed her status on LinkedIn to make it look like she'd left for a new job overseas, then just… disappeared. The kongsi gelap saga and turning Rachel's condo upside down was for our benefit. To make it look like Rachel had been abducted. Just a tale on Nicole's part to keep us off her own tail. And if we inform the authorities about Rachel's disappearance, unlikely they'll do much."

"Pastor Raymond," murmured Philip irrelevantly.

"Meanwhile, Nicole is still quietly carrying on with her humanitarian work with that NGO. And Gerik is very close to the Thai border. Easy to slip out of the country, if need be."

"Not advisable to have her son with her, though. It would be too tough for him," remarked Philip shrewdly. "Poor Cooper, wonder what's happened to the little chap."

Romy said airily, "Oh, there was also another reason Nicole wanted us to go to the condo. I found the boy when I went back there again. He was hiding in one of the handbags. I just looked for a bag wide enough for a cat's whiskers."

"Huh? What lah, you lost me man."

"Aiya, you mean you donno that a cat's whiskers is like a ruler? That's how they know how much space they need to hide in. You were sleeping in Biology class izzit?"

There was the sudden sound of a machine whirring, immediately followed by a startled yowl, and Romy's exasperated, "Oi, Cooper, stop playing with the vacuum cleaner!"

"Aiseh 'My, you mean Cooper is a CAT?!!"

"Ya, lor. Lucky I didn't file a missing person's report. What a dungu I would've looked!"

"Missing purr-son," quipped Philip.

"But his name's too long," Romy went on, oblivious to his friend's attempt at wit. "I think I'll call him Brad instead."

"Bradley Coo-purr," Philip tried again.

"Who? OIC, you mean like the actor." Nope, Romy didn't get that one, either.

But then again, he was also preoccupied with admiring his bank balance on his Mybank4me at the same time.

The numbers on the napkin had proven to be as he'd hoped. A bank account no. and a pin. Enough to feed a contingent of cats, if need be, for a long time.

And if Romy were prudent, some money left over for him too. So he need never feel too poor. Or, should one say… 'pawr'.

5

✕

PI ROMY SEIZES THE DAY

✕

PI Romy couldn't believe his unexpected piece of good luck.

He placed his hands at 9 o'clock and 3 o'clock on the steering wheel and was good to speed.

"I'm a bit pokai at the moment," the portly towkay had said, shamefacedly. "How about you take my SF 90 for a spin, go jolly a while, later I settle your final bill, hor?"

Romy thought for the umpteenth time, how weird rich people were. The towkay was hard pressed to stump out a measly RM500? Yet his stable of cars, other than the Ferrari on offer, included two Lamborghinis, a Maserati and a BMW M8 Coupé. These were just the ones parked in the temporarily impoverished towkay's front porch. God alone knew what other breeds of exotic cars were squirreled away in the basement.

Romy eyed the iron stallion's sleek black torso wistfully. Yet he was hesitant about handling its insane acceleration. Then he thought, heck, what was that quote all those motivational smart asses liked to say?

Carpe diem.

He got into the driver's seat.

"And I bagi lu pinjam my watch, so you don't lose track of the time, huhuhu!" The godfather of a towkay removed his Richard Mille Speedtail with a chubby hand and strapped it securely onto Romy's wrist. "Enjoy!"

The Ferrari seemed to have a will of its own as it roared round the length and breadth of Taman Duta, like a wild iron beast. At the corner of Jalan Tengku Ampuan, its brakes screeching, it turned sharply up into Cangkat Duta, then an about-turn down the steep gradient of Jalan Tunku Putra. Within the space of a minute, it was on the AKLEH headed toward the neighborhood of Taman Zooview.

Romy's ex-wife simply gaped when he drew up outside the gate of her parents' modest bungalow.

"What? You never seen a sports car before, izzit?" remarked Romy loftily.

"Oh, not that," was her scathing reply. "It's just I've never seen *you* in a sports car before."

Romy ground his teeth mentally. Urrgh, it was like her prime purpose in life was to put him down.

"I want to take Aiman for a ride," he told her.

She hesitated before replying. It wasn't Romy's turn to have their son. Besides, she disliked deviation from routine. It was the Teacher in her, adhering to set rules and timetables. Finally, she said, "Aiman's not here. He just left for football practice."

If Romy was disappointed, he was damned if he was going to let that spoilsport see it. He revved up the car engine a few times and let its Pirelli Z4 tyres scorch the entire length of Jalan Lee Woon.

"What was that, Mama?" asked Aiman, entering the kitchen and yawning. "Sounded like a racing car."

"Hmm? Oh, it was just the lori sampah," his mother replied smoothly. "They always make such a racket, and on a Sunday, too."

$$\times$$

It wasn't that Romy was intentionally taking the curves of the DUKE too fast.

There was something not quite stable about the car. It seemed to veer to the left, no matter how firmly Romy gripped the steering wheel in a forward direction.

Shit, was the engine dragging? And why was the amber slow down light suddenly beginning to flash.

Everything happened so quickly.

As the saying went, 'In the blink of an eye, everything can change.'

Romy recalled the car going in a 360 degree spin a couple of times, then a popping sound as it careened over the metal barrier onto the grassy ravine below.

As the car hit the ground turtle, he smelt the petrol fumes.

With the survival instincts of someone who had seen active service in Somalia, Bosnia, Sudan, and for the briefest of periods that he'd almost forgotten, Afghanistan, Romy flung himself out of the burning wreck and rolled away as fast and furiously as he could.

There was a huge bang. A great orange ball of fire licked the grass and swirled upwards in a single magnificent plume of smoke.

Carpe diem, my foot, was his first thought. He'd obviously seized the wrong day.

His next thought was, *yaa Allah, Aiman!*

Then he remembered. He had been in the car on his own. Cautiously, he felt himself for burns and bruises. He'd singed his hair but was more or less okay. But his nose seemed to have doubled in size and burned like hell, though.

The watch on his wrist. It had obviously been thrust on his person for a reason. He yanked it off and flung it into the smoldering flames.

In the distance, he could hear faint exclamations of horrified glee, as the first spectators arrived to gawp at the mini inferno.

Romy snuck away, unseen. He still had enough of his wits about him to know exactly where he was. Gombak.

There were a couple of pals of his in the area, where he could turn up on the doorstep unannounced, and they wouldn't bat an eyelid. It was a fraternity pact only possible amongst ex-mili buddies.

Maybe not yet.

He needed to wrap his head around what was happening. And decide on whose door he was going to knock. *Perhaps not Hanif's*, he decided. The guy had a family and aged parents, all living under the same roof.

Grabbing a 'teh tarik, gula kasi lebih 'dik' from a nearby warung, he tried to look as normal as possible, his cap visor tilted the lowest it could go.

Thank God his mask was still slipped under his chin. Pulling it up to well and truly cover his mouth and nose, he could've been any Uncle Hensem (sic) going jalan-jalan on a beautiful morning. Because outdoor exercise was allowed under the new SOP.

There was always something reassuringly normal about having a teh tarik. Like, at the end of the day, everything would somehow be okeh.

Romy knew he was in shock. But hell, man, he'd survived. Yet again. Even better, that asshole of a towkay assumed he was dead. Which opened up a lot of possibilities. For revenge.

He wasn't sure how, exactly. But ya, he'd figure something out, sap sap sui.

$$\times$$

When Romy rang the bell of his ex-squad mate, Arason Ponalingam (AP for short), smelling of burnt metal and with his nose like a proboscis monkey, Arason declared, "Gimme the name, 'My, and I'll return the favor for you. Rearrange the features on the bugger's face, he will look jerrst like a Picasso installation."

Because AP was arty and high-brow laidat.

"Deyy, seriously?" Romy's question was rhetorical. He hadn't been AP's UNOSOM battle buddy in '93 not to know when AP meant business.

Their nearly ill-fated recce in that Bradley IFV along the dirt road just outside Mogadishu could have so easily bumped up the casualty list. If it hadn't been for AP's eagle eye and Romy's uncanny reflexes.

They'd always had each other's backs. It was a squad thing.

After leaving the army, Arason had become a successful semi-pro boxer. He was a bit of a showman with his flashy punches and karate-like stance. But it meant he could pull in the crowds, so sponsors loved him. The Smiling Assassin, that was his nickname.

But a boxing career had a short expiry date.

AP was now a plumber. And he'd proven to be a damn good one too. It was almost obscene how much money he made looking down people's kitchen sinks and toilet bowls. But AP was one of those who gave his all, in whatever he did. A life coach's dream.

"Hey, you know, 'My," he liked to say, "as Martin Luther King said, if a man sweeps streets for a living, he should sweep those goddamn streets so well, that all the deities of heaven and earth will stop to say, 'Here lived a great street sweeper.'"

"Uh huh," had been Romy's response. Who the heck was Martin Luther King?

But to get back to AP's offer. Romy mentioned a name.

"Oh, dat f'llerr!" AP said derisively, "he's a waste of space. Made so many enemies, snaking his way to the top. But aiyoyo, he must be in deep shit, to wanna use even you as his burnt-out corpse," he added reverently, making it sound almost like a compliment.

"Screw him," Romy retorted. "I just want my car back."

"Get real, lah, Brudder. I bet he's already cannibalized and dumped your car somewhere. The farter's got to get rid of any evidence that you were ever near his place."

What the Freak! His beloved Bezza! Romy tried not to cry.

"Oh, man up!" AP said impatiently. "Or I'll be asking you your bra size. We need to strategize. I have my resources. Meanwhile, you'll hafta lie low. Deffo can't go back to your place till we sort out this crap. As it happens, my cousin brother's brother-in-law is a remisier at that bank next to Zouk. This'll be a hot tip for him, hee hee."

Before Romy could ask, "What's so funny?", AP had eagerly changed the subject, "Now that you mention Zouk –"

"But I didn't," protested Romy.

AP ignored him. "I wanna tell you 'bout this babe I met online last week…"

Romy sighed. *Ah yes,* AP and the 'babes' he was always meeting. AP was no spring chicken. Yet, was there any woman below the age of thirty five on Tinder that he hadn't swiped right?

Romy himself was not in the mood to hear about AP's cyber sex life. All he wanted was his car.

AP saw his sour expression. "Hey, lighten up, Bro. So life's given you lemons, but at least you know whose eyes you can squeeze 'em in."

Romy replied darkly. "Yeah. He tried to have me burnt. I swear I'll watch the bastard fry."

$$\times$$

The following day, which was Monday, the FTSE KLCI closed 15 points or 0.07% lower at an eleven-week low of 1616 points. It was a market made jittery, as a knee-jerk reaction to the towkay's unexpected demise.

ISK stocks, the mega corporation controlled by the late towkay, immediately shed 12% of its market value and was predicted to go into free fall in the coming days, which it did.

Everyone appeared stunned by the news. But underlying the veiled comments of shock and sympathy on the news portals and Twitter, it was obvious how much beef many netizens had with the Towk.

Well, in business, one couldn't just tiptoe to the top, without trampling over everyone else. What inane people who knew nothing about dogs, liked to term a dog eat dog world.

'Dog eat dog'. Such an inappropriate phrase to depict man's best friend. If Romy had to choose, he would've actually preferred a dog over a cat.

But the Muslim consensus was that contact with dogs was haraam – despite the only specific prohibition being that dogs were not to be kept inside the house. Unlike cats.

Cat! Drat, he knew he'd forgotten something. Brad. "Deyy, I need to go home, feed my cat."

"You crazy, man? Let that hairy ball eat the rats in your kitchen. Wait. What, you have A Cat? A CAT?!!"

AP was a good bloke and he had subscriptions not just to Astro and Netflix, but to Mubi, Sooka, Hulu, Britbox and even Squid TV. He also had a cousin aunty's friend's daughter's niece, who worked at Haja Haliq.

But there were only so many action movies Romy could watch and a limit as to the 100 gram packets of murukku he could munch. The cans of lager were another story.

With a tinge of regret, because ya, the sojourn at AP's had been good and helped him get over his recent trauma without rekindling bad old memories, he bade bye bye to his friend.

Daaamn, it was bliss to be coming home. This was his castle.

He loved his 'hood. Ya, orait, parts of it were slummy and downright dodgy, true. But it was considered to be a centrally placed part of KL, with its metropolitan vibe and motley blend of satu Malaysia. Unlike that poncy housing estate where his Abang lived, stuck in the middle of nowhere.

He was about to unlock his front door when his neighbor remarked, "Lomy, lu ada hutang, woi?" Kepochi personified, but Aunty Wong's heart was generally in the right place.

"Huh?"

"Baik jaga-jaga. Ada olang cali lu."

Romy shrugged. Definitely the towkay's macai checking to ensure he'd perished in the fire. Unlikely they'd return. It was a master stroke of his to have thrown the watch into the fire when he did.

AP had also handed him an anonymous SIM card for temporary use till the situation cooled.

Brad's reaction on seeing him was predictable. He just hung about his bowl and miaowed vociferously. Like any cat, he merely regarded Romy as "that ape who brings me my food." Not that he'd been pining while Romy was away. The resourceful little bugger had artfully gnawed through an unopened 5kg pack of Royal Canin and cleverly rationed his water bowl.

Romy watched the stock market slowly correct itself as the week went by. But ISK shares just sunk lower and lower.

AP called him unexpectedly. "Deyy, wanna play stock market?"

"You think I'm mad izzit? I'm still trying hard to figure how to bodek my bank manager to gimme an overdraft. I need a down payment for a car."

"I'll put you in for ten thou," AP replied.

"Where am I going to find ten thou?"

"No sweat, I payung you," AP told him grandly.

Normally Romy would've made a joke of it. But he was too depressed and at a loose end. "I'd rather you make a masterpiece of that towkay's fat face for me," Romy reminded him.

But AP had already hung up.

Romy cursed the bastard of a towkay for the hundredth time. He couldn't risk resuming his usual PI services till the coast was clear.

In the meanwhile, not to unduly alarm his clerk by his absence, he'd texted her using the anonymous number, with the glib excuse that he was in a quarantine center for a couple of weeks.

But all she'd replied was, "Which one?"

Romy mooched about his armpit's width of an apartment. How the time seemed to crawl. Heck, if he had an opportunity even to watch paint dry, he would've done so, he was that bored. *Carpe Duluxem.*

Nobody knew where they came from, but rumors were slowly surfacing that the towkay hadn't perished after all. There was even talk that he was self-isolating off the shores of Langkawi in his yacht. Another rumor had him spotted at a tourist attraction in Batu Gajah. Then there was a viral photo of him in sunglasses and a #kitajagakita face mask, buying carpets in Nilai.

Whatever the rumors swirling around, ISK shares appeared to be gaining ground. Its counter became a hive of activity but nobody was complaining. Not that Romy gave a whistle or a toot. He still harbored hopes of seeing the towkay fried. And possibly getting his Bezza back.

It wasn't much he was asking, he lamented to Brad. But Brad merely assumed one of his haughty stares in Romy's direction, before stretching out a languid paw and yawning widely.

Most nights after 9 pm, to take his mind off his yearning for his car, Romy took to pounding the five foot ways of what he still called Jalan Ipoh.

He recalled with affectionate nostalgia how, decades ago as a podgy recruit, his sergeant had assumed an undisguised loathing toward him.

"Aku kerjakan kau sampai lemak kau melalak!" he would roar, aiming a kick in Romy's direction.

So while the other recruits were let off lightly with a hundred pushups, or, scaling the sand dunes which bordered their barracks thirty times only, Romy had the dubious privilege of being subjected to double the number. *My sweat is my fat crying* became Romy's private mantra.

His nightly runs increased in distance. It was his way of ensuring a sound sleep so he wouldn't lie awake, shedding tears over his beloved Bezza. He made a habit of running all the way up Jalan Ipoh, past Sunway Putra Hotel to the KFC at the crossroads of Jalan Raja Laut and back again.

Romy had fond memories of both the KFC and especially the hotel, when it was known as The Legend. He'd brought Aiman there a few times, to the buffet at the coffee house. There was a chocolate fountain and a range of ice cream flavors, which his then three year-old son absolutely looked forward to.

"Papa, we go makan aiskrim. Pleesh."

Those were happy times.

And it had given his then wife a chance to indulge her Anglophile tastebuds with her favorite Beef Wellington and sticky toffee pudding. Sometimes, there was a sale on at The Mall and he'd treat her to a new Guess handbag or a pair of Marie Claire shoes.

Romy had naively thought those little outings were enough to keep her content. But no.

Apa lagi pompuan mau, haa, he had complained to Philip, after a particularly acrimonious argument over a bottle of Estée Lauder perfume he'd bought her as a surprise. She'd gone on and on about an EDT version having been good enough, even though the EDP one was more expensive and so in Romy's mind, better.

Shit, he really missed his car.

AP messaged him on his fake Insta account.

'Hey wanna go to a party?'

'Nope'

'C'mon man. My csn gf csn sisinlaw bday. Murder mystery theme. Lots of makan n u get to be a detective.'

'Ayam a detective u dungu'.

'Oops. I pick u up at 8. Wear kurta.'

Carpe DM.

Romy didn't know why he indulged his friend. *Because you're a nice guy,* his ego replied, as he removed a stray thread from the collar of his 70% off British India Nehru-style shirt.

The venue was a grandiose bungalow, too large for its land area to appear anything but crass. It was a Malaysian thing. To lack a sense of context and proportion when designing a house. This one had overreached itself. It was as if Tinkerbell had waved her little wand and whisked away Cinderella's castle in Disneyland onto a ten thousand square foot plot of land in Hartamas Heights.

"But they are a very high-class family one," AP pointed out proudly.

The family fortunes, which had resulted in the present display of gilded opulence, had been derived from a chain of goldsmith shops on Lorong Masjid India.

Yet they were magnanimous in their own way, donating generously to welfare homes for the aged, and could always be relied on to contribute toward the renovations of temples in urgent need of repair.

"Sometimes they run their residence as an Air BnB. Give chance to those who want to experience staying in a castle," explained AP. "They've even had guests booking for two weeks at a time."

"Staying for a fortnight?" exclaimed Romy.

"Fort knight! Good one, brudder," chuckled AP.

True to form, Romy didn't geddit.

Parking was anywhere along the side of the road. It was still early but there were already several cars mounted on the pavement close to the, um, castle.

AP's cousin's girlfriend's cousin sister-in-law proved to be a vivacious, willowy beauty in a shimmering emerald colored sari. She was called Dimple. It was evident why, each time her generous lips widened into a smile, which was often.

Her jewellery was minimal. Perhaps the overflowing Kundan and Polki jewellery sets in the window displays of her family's goldsmith shops had resulted in a disinclination toward anything oh tee tee. Just a dainty maang-tikka on her forehead and a pair of Rose ear clips. The single bangle on her slim arm was of a flower blossom, effortlessly enhanced by demantoid garnets and canary diamonds. Very pretty but frankly, in Romy's view, not that women's jewellery was his thang, nothing to shout about.

Despite that, there were loud squeals of "Oh, JAR!" as each of her chums greeted her and scrutinized her unshoutable trinkets.

"JAR!" Romy repeated to himself. It sounded a suitably sardonic response he could use sometime. Preferably on his ex-wife.

At such a party where he knew no one, Romy thought the Covid situation had its pluses. Like, the anonymity afforded by a mask. He kept his steadfastly on. But in next to no time, several guests had impetuously shed theirs. It wasn't that crowded, though.

The SOP relating to numbers allowed for gatherings had been strictly adhered to.

All the same, Romy was careful to keep a social distance and to lower his mask only when enjoying his club soda & lime or chowing down. But some fat slob still managed to spill a tankard of Kia Kaha! sparkly on his carefully laundered gray cotton sleeve.

Romy was pissed off, it was bound to leave a stain. But before he could protest, the fei chai had buggered off.

As AP had confidently predicted, there was plenty of food. And it was good. "All specially catered from Nadodi," informed AP. "Just been voted one of Asia's 50 best restaurants."

Romy wasn't surprised. The spinach & lentils kootu was like no other. And it seemed to be a marriage made in heaven, paired with the coconut rosematta rice.

"Now I've tried all this, how am I ever going to be satisfied eating at Bala's Banana Leaf again?" he grumbled jokingly, as he piled on another helping of Hokkaido shellfish fritters done intriguingly in Kerala style.

Dimple overheard him. "PI Romy, control your tempura please!" she giggled.

Suddenly, the chandelier lights were dimmed.

There was an expectant hush from all the guests.

A sepulchral, disembodied voice announced, "Maharajahs & Maharanees, Nawabs & Begums, Mahodeys & Mahilas, Sahibs & Memsahibs, may I present.. A Murder."

There was a spine-chilling, high-pitched scream.

A few of the women giggled nervously, the agony in its tone had sounded so authentic.

An extended, awkward belly laugh emanated from one of the men.

Later, Romy recalled, the overhead spotlight had swirled round the faces of each of the pseudo bemused guests that fraction too long.

So bright was its beam that Romy felt almost blinded, before the light came to rest on a fat figure, swinging lifelessly on the champagne and pink Baccarat chandelier, bang in the center of the hall.

While his facial features had not been completely obliterated, in a macabre way the contorted result was almost artistic. There were huge scorch marks on his clothing and the visible area of skin revealed by his embroidered dupion silk sherwani was charred to the bone.

Romy caught his breath sharply. This was deffo not going according to the usual murder mystery party script.

Everyone else suddenly realized it too. Genuine screams of shock and horror reverberated round the castle walls.

AP whispered in the chaos that followed, "'Kay, 'My. Perut kenyang oredi. Partay's over. Time to cabut."

As the car sped along Jalan Kuching and beyond, onto what AP also continued to call out of habit Jalan Ipoh, he remarked casually, "KL so small, lah. But still got quite a crowd at the party tonight."

Romy didn't beat about the bush. "His face. Was it your handiwork?"

AP was non-committal. "Like I said, 'My, the wanker had a lot of enemies."

"Ya," Romy agreed. "And one of them really wanted to see him fried." He added thoughtfully. "Wonder what the autopsy report will state."

"Cardiac arrest, I should think."

AP was right.

The towkay's primary cause of death was a myocardial infarction. It was also unfortunate he was suffering from several other underlying health issues.

Apparently he had suffered a sudden shock, which unfortunately triggered a severe heart attack. And it was also equally unfortunate that he had then toppled backward into the industrial-sized tandoor oven in the courtyard. The pictures of him strung up among the lights, which had popped up on social media, were just what was termed officially, "deep fake and had no basis whatsoever."

Romy remembered the incident of the spilled Kia Kaha! sparkly.

Heck, if the tables had been turned, and he had been on the other end, he would most likely have had a heart attack, too.

$$\times$$

AP called him a few days later. "Were you following the stock market?"

"Heck, no. Why would I?"

"I payung you that ten thou, remember?"

Nope, Romy didn't.

"It was for ISK shares. Sold them just before the party. Made enough for a deposit for a couple of new cars. A Perodua Ativa for you and an X1 for me."

Of course, Romy appreciated AP's generosity. But touchy feely was not in his emotional vocabulary. "You dumbass," he said disparagingly, as a term of endearment. Then added, puzzled, "Eh, Perodua has an X1 model?"

"BMW X1, lah."

"JAR!" retorted Romy, for good measure, just to bring his friend down a peg or two.

6

$$\times$$

PI ROMY SEES THE BIG PICTURE

$$\times$$

PI Romy checked his weight on the scales in his bedroom and sighed.

Absolutely no more snacking, he told himself sternly. It was only the fifth day of Raya and he had alreadly put on two kay gee. This was crazy considering he hadn't been out visiting, not even to Mak's.

He was also aggrieved that for the first time ever, when he had a new car to flash to his ex-commandant on the pretext of dropping by to salam Raya, he couldn't. At the risk of being captured by a drone for noncompliance of the SOP.

Sial betul.

A drone, for God's sake! What had the state of the country come to! Two decades on and Romy could still recall the drones that whirred in the skies on that long, futile yomp from Kabul to Kandahar.

He shuddered.

No point dwelling on those memories. They sure as hell weren't going to help him shed that unwanted Two Kay Gee.

To console himself, he reached for his stash of kuih kapit. Aunty Wong, who lived two doors across, was 81 years old but still insisted on occasionally making kuih kapit as gifts for, "gua suka, gua bagi."

Last one, Romy vowed after five minutes of continuous munching. The tin was empty, anyway.

He skimmed through the details of his interstate travel permit, which had arrived by courier a few minutes before. It would be good to get out of KL for a while. And this particular assignment seemed the nearest to a holiday.

Someone on his regular PI chat group had put it out there if anyone was keen to take on a short stint as minder to some high baller out in the sticks. The exact location was not divulged. While others had hemmed and hawed and insisted on more deets, Romy had simply keyed in, 'K on!' when he read the message.

Oh gawd. As usual, he'd almost forgotten about Brad.

In the end, he arranged with Aunty Wong to help feed the chairman meow. Once every couple of days should suffice.

"Gua kasi lu makan satu kali dalam dua hali, tengok lu boleh tahan, woi!" she told Romy off severely. "Gua kasi dia lua kali makan sehali," she declared firmly. Then, peering at him more closely through her black-rimmed glasses, she added, "Waa, lu hali laya ini tahun manyak enjoy maa. Sudah mau nampak gumuk, lor!"

Romy decided against cadging her for another tin of kuih kapit for his journey.

He wondered what this coming assignment was about. Probably a humdrum routine of soothing an oofy old dude's paranoiac fears. He hoped it wasn't too much to expect his own room. Barrack life and then later, married life, had made him jealous about guarding his space.

But the fact that this time he was being picked up by helicopter to get to his job location augured well. It could so easily have been that he had to bus it from Terminal Bas Pekeliling to wherever. His new Ativa was too precious to risk a road trip.

The instruction was that he had to be at the helipad at 3pm. 'Wear a white shirt. You will be asked the question, if the world was ending, you'd come over, right? Your reply must be correct.'

Just like a spy movie, thought Romy wryly. Rich people were so weird.

The helipad was on the rooftop of what used to be called the Promet building but was now known as something else. Promet. *Heck*. Romy suddenly realized he was that old, to still remember when Promet was the darling of the KL Stock Exchange. Not to mention the flamboyant Tan Sri who was so integral to the company, that Promet itself got tacked onto his name.

The bird was on the tarmac.

Romy noted with a wowsome expression that it was a Sikorsky S-76. He tried not to swagger as he mounted the electrically extendable steps.

The uniformed flight attendant by the large, limousine-like cabin doors greeted him deferentially, "Welcome aboard, Encik Romy."

Romy nodded.

"If the world was ending, you'd come over, right?" The attendant assumed a conversational tone.

Romy thought for a moment before answering slowly, "Correct."

The female honeypot pilot is probably a double agent, mused Romy jokingly to himself, as he reclined his plush velvet seat into a comfortable position. There was a posh totty look about her, as his ex-wife would say.

All the previous 'copters Romy had traveled in had been noisy, rattling, ugly things. This one was so quiet and smooth, it was as comfortable as being on a plane. No expense had been spared in kitting it out, either. *Come on, man. Hermès cushion headrests.*

The attendant brought him a cold towel and asked if he would like a dash of vodka in his freshly squeezed orange juice.

"I never drink when I fly," Romy replied priggishly. "But if you can bring me some nuts, it would be nice."

The attendant obliged immediately with a bowl of salted cashews. Romy felt he was on cloud nine.

He regretted not being able to take selfies to show Aiman but he was on official business. Romy was professional laidat.

A sudden wind sprang up, which made the landing several minutes later slightly choppy.

According to his observations and calculations of the flight path, they were somewhere in the upper reaches of Cameron Highlands. *Further north of Brinchang, more toward Tringkap*, he reckoned.

Rain was falling in a steady drizzle as Romy hurried across the wide expanse of lawn to the verandah, along the side of the imposing colonial-style house.

The houseboy, who was hovering by the potted palms, immediately rushed out with an umbrella to the attendant, and relieved him of his briefcase at the same time. Romy noticed it was a Dunhill Heritage Slim. *Heck.* Rich people were deffo weird.

"I'm sorry, I didn't realize… you… er, um… Datuk Seri," he apologized to the 'attendant'. He hadn't expected his employer to be so young.

"Oh, I'm Sam. Datuk Seri Hasnul is my father," chuckled the young man. "And the pilot, Astrid – she's my sister. The James Bond touch at the start was just one of our quirks. We're all mad here."

Romy wasn't sure how to respond to that.

Sam saw his discomfiture. "Let me show you to your room," he said cheerfully.

To Romy's relief it was comfortable, albeit sparsely furnished. It even had its own attached bathroom.

"Feel free to wander round the house as you please. Except we prefer the upstairs to be reserved only for our immediate family. Astrid is especially territorial about that." Sam glanced at Romy's obviously under-packed Kathmandu rucksack. "There are clothes in the wardrobe you can wear. You look about the same size as the chap you're standing in for. Dinner is at 8. Ayah is a stickler for punctuality."

He left the room, whistling a few bars of a tune.

Sure enough, there were several neatly pressed clothes hanging in the wardrobe and a few personal toiletries on the chest of drawers. Romy assumed they must belong to the minder he was filling in for.

That was another plus. Romy had only brought one change of clothes and an extra pair of boxers to use as pyjamas.

$$\times$$

When the mahogany grandfather clock in the hallway struck the hour at 8, Romy found himself seated at dinner in the long elegant dining room with Datuk Seri Hasnul and his family.

There was a large silver tureen of rice and several dishes laid on the table. The same houseboy earlier served the good Datuk Seri his food. The others were expected to take turns to serve each other and themselves, from the dishes nearest to them. From time to time, one of the kitchen staff would enter noiselessly to replenish the dishes where necessary and to clear away the plates for the next course.

Datin Seri Juwita smiled graciously at Romy. "I wish the weather could've been more considerate when you arrived."

She was a handsome woman in her sixties. But as was usual amongst many ladies past their prime, she carried more weight than necessary round her waist.

Her husband was several years older, distinguished-looking, with a narrow, aristocratic face. He was of that rare breed, having inherited his vast wealth without any reliance on political patronage. Prior to his retirement, the good Datuk Seri had been a career diplomat. Astrid, their daughter, had been born in Norway, hence her name. Romy noted she walked with a slight limp.

There was another son, Rizz. Good-looking like his brother Sam, but taciturn.

They seemed a normal family. Romy would even go further to describe them as nice people.

A nephew and niece were living with them too.

Datin Seri remarked on their absence. "Jake and Fenny not dining with us tonight?"

The houseboy replied. "Mister Jake playing his new game online. Resident Evil Village. He tell me bring dinner to his room."

Romy recalled hearing haptic sounds coming from the room next to his. So that was what it was.

"Fenny claims she has a stomachache," volunteered Sam. "She says it was the ikan patin tempoyak we had last night."

"But we all ate the same food," Datuk Seri expressed his surprise.

"Perhaps it'll be a chance for her to lose weight," murmured Astrid. "Except she's always saying she's obese because Pak Ngah and Mak Ngah are obese. And Jake also happens to be obese."

"It sounds like obesity runs in her family," Romy commented politely.

Rizz, who had so far said nothing, remarked dryly, "It sounds like nobody runs in her family."

His mother chided him mildly, "Is that a kind thing to say about your relatives?" She turned to Romy. "PA Romy, may I offer you more rice?"

"Oh, no thank you, Datin Seri."

Frankly, Romy would have enjoyed another helping of rice. The cool highland air had whetted his appetite. But the company at dinner was so urbane and refined, he felt lumpish beside them.

He was also acutely conscious that he had, as usual, forgotten to take his damask napkin from its repoussé silver holder to place on his lap. So it lay there, the only one still on the table, as glaringly singular as the final strand of hair atop a bald man's head.

A maid brought in the dessert, and also assisted the houseboy in clearing away the plates from the main course.

"The strawberries in the trifle are from our garden," Datin Seri Juwita informed Romy proudly. "I grow the vines myself."

Her husband patted her arm indulgently. "Dewiku. My angel has green fingers," he said to Romy.

"I must take you on a tour of our garden tomorrow, PA Romy," offered the Datin Seri eagerly. "I can wear my new hat. And if it's a fine day, we may walk through the park afterward, to the high street. I love browsing round that lovely farmers' market behind Newcombe House, which sells the freshest produce, all of it organic."

Astrid said, "I'll go with you, Mama. We can get those Pinkerton avocados you like so much, to make guacamole."

Rizz spoke for the second time that evening. "Stop layaning Mama, Astrid."

"But I'm merely making plans with Mama for tomorrow," retorted his sister.

"Just leave them be, Rizzo," Sam said, coming to Astrid's defense.

"Make a new plan, Stan," countered Rizz scornfully.

"No need to be coy, Roy," Astrid shot back.

"Oh, go hop on a bus, Gus," her brother snapped.

"It's basically a nonsense song," their father interjected patiently, easing the unexpected tension which had suddenly sprung up among the siblings. "I think avocados are a splendid idea. The potassium and folates in them will be good for Mama."

Romy was suddenly aware they were speaking as though the Datin Seri were not there. Unexpectedly, she caught his eye and smiled ruefully. She looked very vulnerable. Romy felt sorry for her.

She must have noted that, because with the dignity of her generation who eschewed pity, she declared, completely changing the subject, "It's abominable, those dreadful air strikes happening in Gaza now. All that senseless killing with impunity."

"They call it 'mowing the grass', Mother." Rizz's tone was curiously devoid of any emotion.

"For what it's worth, I see cousin Fenny's updated her status, in solidarity against the atrocities going on," observed Sam sardonically.

"All too easy to decry brutality on one's Facebook account, when one is thousands of miles safely away," was his sister's withering comment.

Romy wondered idly what contribution, if any, the toffee-nosed Astrid herself had made toward the Palestinian humanitarian effort.

"Why can't we all just play parlor games and be nice to each other?" suggested the Datuk Seri jovially.

Romy thought, *Blow me down, the old man can't be serious.*

But he was.

Rich people were confirmedly weird.

✕

Romy was about to wonder if breakfast was also a family affair, when there was a discreet knock on his door at 8 am.

The houseboy entered bearing a tray of cut fresh fruit, cereal, poached eggs on toast, apple juice and freshly brewed coffee.

"Datuk Seri say he want to see you in his study after you finish eat," he informed Romy, his mellifluous Bangladeshi accent sounding as though he were awaiting an opportune moment to burst into a rendition of *Kuch Kuch Hota Hai.*

Romy ate as quickly as he could, so as not to keep his employer waiting.

The Datuk Seri's study was at the front of the house. A maid was discreetly arranging a large vase of fresh orchids on the circular marble-top table in the foyer, while another was carefully polishing the antique hardware of the massive cengal wood double front doors.

Romy passed the Datin Seri who was on her way out to the garden. "Nice morning for a walk, Datin Seri," he remarked politely.

She smiled vaguely at him. She was adjusting the brim of her large straw hat before the oval Venetian mirror by the powder room and her face was obscured.

Romy knocked discreetly on the mahogany-paneled study door before entering. The room was generously proportioned but north-facing, which meant it didn't get much light. This was likely intentional as it was a veritable antiquarian book lover's dream, sunlight being an anathema to the preservation of old books.

Its soaring custom-made bookcases were filled with rows and rows of exquisitely bound gilt-edged leather tomes. Several more modern collections also took pride of place, including the complete works of Aldous Huxley and Jean-Paul Sartre, a signed set of John Le Carré novels, a first edition of Agatha Christie's *Five Little Pigs* and, whimsically, a hand-engraved book of illustrations from Lewis Carroll's *Alice in Wonderland*.

There were also some rare Malay manuscripts carefully preserved in a climate-controlled glass cabinet. Romy recognized a century-old copy of Raja Ali Haji's *Tuhfat al-Nafis* as well as a fragment of the famed Malay Annals, painstakingly handwritten in Jawi script. He wished his late father could have viewed these. Arwah Abah had been an avid reader of Sastera Nusantara.

The Datuk Seri was at his desk, writing notes laboriously in a journal. "I'm a dinosaur when it comes to technology," he admitted. "I even avoid using a mobile phone." He went on to ask politely, "I trust you slept well, PI Romy?"

"Ya, " Romy replied.

There was an expectant pause.

"Thank you, Datuk Seri," he added, just in time. Then, emboldened by his hearty breakfast, he asked, "What exactly am I being hired to do?"

Datuk Seri Hasnul took his time before replying. "PI Romy, do you believe in evil?"

Heck, not one of those 'Are you an angel or an arsehole' personality type quizzes, puhleeze, groaned Romy inwardly. Aloud, he replied. "I don't know how true it is, Datuk Seri. But I've heard it said, a lot of evil happens because good people who can do something to stop it, decide to do nothing."

His employer looked at him keenly. "Ah yes. I was informed you've seen some active service, PI Romy. Or it's actually Leftenan Romy, am I right? It was very tragic, in Bosnia, what happened to your fellow officers."

So the good DS had dug deep when doing his homework. "Yes, it was." Romy's tone was one of indifference. "Tragic." He paraphrased his original question. "What is it you want me to investigate that your family mustn't know about, Datuk Seri? I know Datin Seri assumes I'm just your new personal assistant and probably, so do the rest."

Datuk Seri Hasnul sighed and waited several seconds before answering. "As you suggested, PI Romy, a lot of evil can be avoided, if those who are in a position to do so, prevent it from happening. Then again, the capacity to commit evil is inherent in all of us. We may not think so but it slumbers within our souls. Deeper in some souls than others."

The topic of Evil was obviously a hobby horse of the good Datuk Seri. *He likely has nightmares about it a lot of the time*, deduced Romy.

"Something is triggered," Datuk Seri went on. He seemed to be half-talking to himself. "It could be a change in one's circumstances, a missed opportunity, perhaps, or someone else's good fortune. And the evil twists upwards and outwards and is manifested in a deed so abhorrent, execrable, repugnant, that it doesn't bear even uttering a word about."

Big words. And Romy was, frankly, hard pressed to know what the codger was on about.

He wished the scholarly Datuk Seri would just spit it out in plain language, whatever it was he wanted to say. He smoothed a crease on the sleeve of his Giordano linen half placket shirt. Actually it wasn't his, but one of the several pieces of clothing hanging in the wardrobe in his room.

A sudden thought struck him. "Datuk Seri, uh, where's your PA now?"

"Rauf?" The Datuk Seri expressed surprise. "He went back to his hometown just before Ramadhan. A family emergency. They run a floating restaurant at Taman Negara. He was in such a rush, he asked one of the others to inform me after he'd left."

"I see."

Romy was familiar with Taman Negara. He'd taken Aiman trekking to Lata Berkoh a couple of times during the school holidays, and once they'd even made their leisurely way as far as Melantai. Unlikely any of the restaurants were open. Several had rolled up their mats permanently even before the start of the second MCO. It had been the influx of foreign tourists that had kept them afloat in the good years.

"He worked with Datuk Seri for long?"

"About four months. I expect he will be back soon. We are already nearly a week into Syawal."

To Romy's relief, Datuk Seri Hasnul finally spat it out. "PI Romy, I think something evil is about to be committed by someone in my family. Call it instinct or paranoia on my part, I can't pinpoint what exactly, or by whom. It may even be murder. But I need you to prevent it from happening."

Ya, so I'm right, thought Romy. The usual rich man's drama minggu ini. But he couldn't exactly vocalize his sentiments to the good Datuk Seri. Instead, he chewed his lower lip and looked at the slate gray anthropomorphic form of the Anglepoise lamp on the Datuk Seri's desk. Then he let his gaze travel past the window and into the garden.

The gardener was pruning the ixora hedges in the distance. A young boy was helping to pick up the cuttings and tossing them

into a wheelbarrow. In her oversized straw hat, the figure of the Datin Seri was visible, supervising them both.

A yellow-vented bulbul could be heard, warbling its distinctive bubbly calls to its mate. From a nearby tree, a silver-eared mesia trilled its sweet, whistling song. It was a reassuringly idyllic, almost alpine setting. If this were a movie, any moment now the Datin Seri would be flinging her arms out wide in rapture and singing about the hills being alive with the sound of music. The mere notion of any nefarious activities being planned amidst such Arcadian surroundings was absurd.

Nevertheless, Romy enquired politely, "So whom among your family members is it that you suspect, Datuk Seri?" His tone was neutral, as though he were asking something as banal as how many sugars the good DS wanted in his tea.

$$\times$$

The Datuk Seri always partook of lunch in the solitary splendor of his study.

Everyone else had theirs at their leisure, buffet style, in the conservatory.

According to the houseboy, whose name Romy finally discovered was Waheed, the daily lunch menu selection veered toward the cosmopolitan.

"Macam-macam ada," he pointed out proudly to Romy. "Today, got have melon & walnut salad, minestrone soup, butternut risotto, selection of Indian roti and saag. Dessert is apple Charlotte. But some time, also serving donburi, fruits de la mer, bratkartoffeln, sngor chruak sach trei (*heck, the guy sounded like a linguist!*) lechem mishneh, bachy soletanche —"

"Oi, kau ingat aku bodoh, ke?" Romy interrupted him indignantly. "Itu Bachy Soletanche kompeni yang bikin MRT."

"Sori, boss!" Waheed grinned widely and skipped nimbly away, as a well-endowed young woman bustled in.

She made a beeline for the paratha, at the same time addressing Romy, "Oh, you must be my uncle's new clerk." There was no mistaking the condescension in her tone.

"Miss Fenny, izzit?" Romy was careful to exude a subservient tone.

She looked gratified. "Yes, I am she. I heard you telling off that Waheed. That's the way to deal with all these foreign workers. So damn lazy, the lot of them. Say they want to come to Malaysia to work but instead, just sleep here all the time. Alhamdulillah, there's myself around to make sure they don't slack."

She lifted the lid of the chafing dish with a clatter as, with something like awe, Romy watched her pile up her plate with gargantuan quantities of food. His portion, though substantial because everything looked so tantalizing, was midget-sized beside hers.

"Do you know Rauf well, Miss Fenny?" he asked, using her reference to his predecessor as an opening nip.

She looked at him as if he were a couple of curry puffs short of a picnic. Romy took it as a No. It was obvious she had no intention of getting to know him, either.

Sam sauntered in, whistling as usual. Astrid strolled in shortly after, followed by Rizz and a gormless, horizontally challenged youth clutching an iPad, who was obviously Jake.

"Ohh, Kak Astrid," shrilled Fenny guiltily. "I thought you all had eaten already. Sorry, I finished the roti."

"No worries Fen, it's a naan issue," her cousin replied in a bored tone.

"It's naan of my business yup yup, but you're putting on a lot of weight, hey Fenny," Sam chortled.

"Do we really need to discuss the elephant in the room, this minute?" interposed Rizz, adding fat to the fire.

Fenny said nothing but the red spot on each of her cheeks bore testimony to her humiliation. Jake merely snickered and hastily set aside an extra large helping of apple Charlotte with lashings of whipped cream for himself before that, too, was all gone.

Romy addressed everyone conversationally, "Datin Seri already had her lunch?"

"Mama's having one of her turns today," Astrid replied. "I got Chef to make some bubur ayam for Mama."

An in-house chef, observed Romy. No wonder the food was on par with five star hotel standards.

"It must have been because of too much gardening this morning," he remarked chattily.

A look of concern crossed Fenny's plump face. Astrid was frowning as she keyed in a message on her phone and didn't hear him.

"Aiseh, 'bang, you a gamer?" Romy suddenly realized Jake was addressing him through a mouthful of risotto.

"Uhh, no," he replied, "but my son likes to play For Honor sometimes."

"Oh, I like that one too. Isagiyoku shine! Accept it and die!" Jake made some swishing movements with an imaginary sword and gave a high-pitched giggle.

Mental, Romy muttered inwardly to himself but managed a faux smile. Sam was right. They were a bunch of loonies, the whole lot of them.

✕

The excellent lunch had made Romy sleepy.

A nice little lie down seemed like a superb idea. Reclining his head on the feather-filled pillows on the bed, he could listen once more to the discreet recording he had made during the Datuk Seri's discussion with him that morning.

But first, he really ought to seek out the chef and offer his compliments on such a delicious meal. Romy was already fantasizing as to what dinner would be that night.

The chef became almost emotional at Romy's praise. It was obvious his culinary efforts were generally taken for granted.

"Except Rauf. He always tell me he like my food."

"He talk to you often, then?" Romy could see that the Cambodian chef was very lonely. From their conversation, he learned that the chef was from Kampong Cham province, and had not been back home in three years.

"Yes, he very kind young man. That's why I so surprise he don't tell me he go on leave. He say he just going out for a walk."

"I see."

Romy moseyed back to his room in a contemplative mood. The Datin Seri was obviously feeling better as the outline of her figure was visible, coming down the stairs.

He turned on the recording.

'Everyone is capable of evil, PI Romy.. We ourselves are guilty of it but to a lesser degree. That careless jibe simply to make a person feel small… the thoughtless act… the unnecessary unkindness…'

But murder, Romy said to himself. *Here, in this green and pleasant land?*

What else was it the Datuk Seri had mentioned?

'Datin Seri has been missing a lot of her things. I have, too. So strange. Like, for instance, my 16th century katana sword in the display cabinet. Suddenly, it's gone.'

Surely the saga of the missing things was straightforward enough. Probably one of the servants.

But the Datuk Seri was insistent that it was not. His staff were more than amply paid and had been with the family for many years. There was no reason for them to steal. It had to be an outsider: a highland hobo, probably, or a hard-up delivery boy, who'd been quietly casing the joint each time he came by to send a package.

'Theft, bribery, corruption. Those vices are born of poverty and the necessity to survive. Look at Norway, Denmark, New Zealand, PI Romy. Their crime rates are the lowest in the world. Because their governments provide amply for their citizens' welfare, so there's little reason for them to steal. If there were fewer poor people in our country, crime rates would go down too. It's poverty, PI Romy, poverty, which drives our fellow Malaysians to steal.'

Who am I to disagree, Romy said silently to himself, *Bossku.*

The Datuk Seri got on another of his hobby horses.

'I don't believe in holding on to what I have till I die. I can't bring it with me. It's so pointless to die rich, wouldn't you say, PI Romy? I'm already planning to divide and distribute my assets among my family and loved ones while I'm still alive and in full control of my senses.'

The 'low battery' sign flashed across Romy's phone screen. He was about to take out his charger from his rucksack when he saw there was already a charger conveniently plugged into the wall socket above the table.

There were also one or two things idly lying around on the table surface.

This Rauf fellow seemed a very tidak apa sort of chap. *Which PA worth his salt ever forgets to bring his laptop when he goes away?*

$$\times$$

Dinner exceeded Romy's expectations.

He had never tasted such fragrant biryani rice. Apparently the variety of rice in this instance wasn't the usual Basmati or Jasmine but cultivated only in a certain district in Kerala.

"It's called kaima rice, cooked in a claypot over a slow fire and the top of the pot is sealed with wheat dough," Datin Seri Juwita explained. "It takes absolutely ages but that's how the aroma of the herbs and spices are maximized."

She still looked slightly peaky but was otherwise as animated as the evening before. "Oh I rested all day, PA Romy, so I'm much better, thank you. It was just a touch of vertigo," she replied amiably, in response to his courteous question.

But the convivial atmosphere of the previous evening had been replaced with a tautness in the air. An inexplicable awareness of foreboding. Everyone seemed on edge. Or to borrow a French phrase, on le qui vive.

Astrid was surreptitiously checking her phone.

"No phones at the dinner table, please," her mother announced, with what sounded like mock severity.

Putting the forbidden item away, Astrid remarked playfully, "Or you'll take it away from me, Mama?"

"Sam, you're not wearing your Patek Philippe," observed the Datuk Seri suddenly.

Sam looked at his mother keenly before turning to answer his father. "My Calatrava? I seem to have misplaced it."

"Atok will be so upset to hear that," decried the Datin Seri. This time there was no mistaking the vexed note in her voice. "He gave it to you on your 18th birthday, specially."

"Ma, he's been dead more than ten years, I don't think it matters," Rizz remarked pointedly, an undercurrent of bitterness in his tone.

"Still jello 'cos Atok only got you an Omega for your 18th?" taunted Sam.

"Shut up, I already own ten other watches," snapped his brother.

"Oh my, what a lot of time you have on your hands," drawled Fenny boldly, entering into the fray.

Jake snickered and helped himself to more mango acar.

But the reaction from her three cousins to her comment was unexpected and staggering.

They glared at her. More than that. The fury in their eyes was palpable almost to the point of being demonic. It was as though she had stepped way out of some imaginary line.

Romy wondered if perhaps there was some truth in Sam's seemingly flippant remark about madness in the family. He couldn't fathom why the siblings were, as his ex-wife would put it, getting their knickers in a twist over such a mundane remark.

Their mother attempted tactfully to diffuse the situation.

"I've been losing my things too," she admitted sheepishly. "Recently, it was my – my Chouberon? – Boucheron? – onyx and diamond brooch. Last week, it was my Oli Mohamed aquamarine earrings. Now, I can't find my favorite malachite necklace." The corners of her mouth went down in a petulant gesture. "I did so want to wear my necklace tonight."

"All this talk of your 'things'!" teased her husband, gently patting her arm. "You'll never find the right things by looking in the wrong places. Besides, they're just that, manjaku. Things."

"But I Like My Things!" retorted his wife peevishly. "All my friends have their things too, so why can't I?"

She sounded just like a spoilt child. *Heck, women are all the same*, concluded Romy.

"It's called conspicuous consumption, Mama," explained Astrid. "Very 80s."

"Yeah, like Ronald Reagan, 'E.T. phone home', the Eurythmics and all that spandex," said Sam.

"Tetris and Pac-man," piped up Jake eagerly. "Oh, and Freddie Krueger."

"It's not cool, Ma," Sam went on. "We do minimalism now."

"A bit late to introduce Mama to minimalism at her stage in life, don'tcha think?" quizzed Rizz mockingly.

Sam replied swiftly, "Bro, it's the least we can do."

The others chuckled.

No, he didn't get it. But Romy was relieved to find the atmosphere back to normal.

The Datin Seri smiled at him conspiratorially. She said deliberately, in a tone meant for his ears only, "PI Romy, you must find us such a strange family."

So the Datin Seri had known all along. Her impeccant expression made him uneasy. Perhaps it was her hooded eyes.

At the same time, one of the others at the table had overheard her and was obviously rattled.

Gotcha, Romy said to himself, feeling quite chuffed by his powers of deduction.

Yet… common thief, yes, but intending to go so far as commit murder?

Best I sleep on it before jumping to any hasty conclusions, he decided. There were still a couple more pieces required to complete the puzzle.

$$\times$$

Romy passed a restless night. In the realm between waking and sleeping and waking again, snatches of the conversation at dinner came back to him.

"Atok will be so upset to hear that –"

"Ma, he's been dead more than ten years –"

"I seem to be losing my things –"

'Some of them want to use you..

Some of them want to abuse you…' (No, that was from a song)

"– you'll take it away from me? –"

"– and Freddie Krueger –"

"You'll never find the right things by looking in the wrong places –"

'Who am I to disagree –' (That song again)

"– and Freddie Krueger –"

"– I thought he just go out for a walk –" (Nope, that was a different conversation, altogether)

"– 'ET phone home' –"

It was a relief when his phone alarm chimed 'Radar', indicating it was time to get up.

He really needed to go for a pre-breakfast run. Especially as Waheed had mentioned that Chef did the best Singapore fried meehoon for breakfast on Wednesdays.

It was still fairly dark, though, as there was nearly an hour to go before syuruk. But his headlight was strapped securely to his forehead and his trusty Merrells had never let him down.

He'd heard the surrounding area made for some breathtaking nature trails and in anticipation, had installed the latest magnetometer app in his phone.

Man, it was so good to be trail-running again after so long. The last time had been in Maliau, a few months before that Covid shit happened, and was still happening. Romy inhaled a lungful of fresh mountain air and felt an inexplicable sense of elation. It was just a runner's high, as he still hadn't cracked the case. *But damn. The joy of exercise.*

The forest was almost rambunctious with the sound of activity. From the ear-splitting chorus of cicadas competing for first dibs to snag a mate, to the incessant nasally twitter of the spiderhunter as it flitted among the cluster of flowering vines, and not forgetting the siamang's distinct call, which sounded like a cross between an ambulance siren and a squeaky balloon.

It was like one big noisy jungle-themed party.

As he made his way back to the house, the sun was shining in between the puffy white balls of cumulus clouds and he was able to put away his headlight.

He hadn't realized the property was so isolated. There were hairpin bends and potholes all along the way up, not to mention the verge between road and precipice was as narrow as Brooke Shields' midriff. Yeah, Romy was also very '80s in his own way.

As he continued running, he was reminded of his recent tumble, out of a seemingly rebellious Ferrari.

His thoughts seemed to be disjointed.

So much so, he nearly tripped over a small rock protruding among the tufts of sparse wild grass. A further misstep and he would have catapulted down a sheer slope. Nobody would have thought to look for him past the layers of rainforest canopy, in the forest floor. The rugged beauty of the landscape cloaked danger at every turn.

Just like the calm waters of Sungai Tembeling.

"Papa, that's a fine-looking log."

"It's a crocodile, Aiman."

On closer inspection, it wasn't a rock which Romy had tripped on. But a broken handle of some sort of ancient artefact. He carried it back with him thoughtfully.

As it was such a beautiful morning, he decided to have his breakfast al fresco, on the little patio outside his room. Man, he could so get used to this.

He was suddenly inspired, as he sipped his glass of freshly blended soursop juice, to send a somewhat belated Raya greeting to the boatman at Kuala Tahan. There was also something he wanted to ask him, and Hari Raya was for a month anyway. *Nice fellow, Pak Kassim, the dearth of tourists must have hit his livelihood hard.*

Damn Covid.

So immersed was Romy in his syllogistic reasoning, he was barely aware how delicious the meehoon tasted.

It was the same with the fluffy pancakes. To his surprise, he realized he'd eaten the whole stack. There was still some maple syrup left in the miniature glass beaker. Bad habit to waste food. He glugged it down.

Indulge and bulge. Oh dear. So much for all the calories burned during his run.

His phone pinged, indicating a reply from Pak Kassim. It was a lengthy one. The gregarious old man had obligingly attached a couple of photos as well.

It was as Romy had feared.

Resignedly, he brushed his teeth and went to report to the Datuk Seri.

Just before that, though, he needed to ask Chef a bit more about Rauf's intended walk and with whom.

Perhaps, he also decided, it would be pragmatic to put in a call to the OCPD at the Balai Polis Tanah Rata.

$$\times$$

"There are drug treatments that may reduce Datin Seri's symptoms temporarily," suggested Romy to his employer.

Datuk Seri Hasnul shook his head. "My bidadari wouldn't want that. There remains no cure and no treatment as yet for Alzheimer's. I accept it will be a long goodbye. Akin to mourning for a loved one who is still alive. But Fenny, on the other hand. To take advantage of her Mak Chor's vulnerability! Datin Seri is so kind to her. I too am kind to her. It's unforgivable what she did. How did you find out, PI Romy?"

"I saw her wearing Datin Seri's hat. They are about the same build. So it would be easy for her to slip upstairs each time Datin Seri was on her own, without anyone realizing. Then sweet talk her way into getting her Mak Chor to 'give' her things. Datin Seri's condition means she would forget soon after, that she'd done so. As for Encik Sam's watch, it came to me from a chance remark by

Cik Astrid, when Datin Seri disapproved of her using her phone at the dinner table. Datin Seri had likely taken his watch away from him recently for some perceived misdemeanor, and put it down somewhere within plain sight, for Fenny to steal."

Datuk Seri chuckled. "Yes, my beloved was strict with the children when they were young. Her method of punishment was to confiscate their belongings and keep them on her dressing table. And with her current condition, it slips her mind that they left their childhood behind a long while ago."

Romy went on. "I realized Fenny wasn't meant to be up there when I mistook her for Datin Seri, as she was coming downstairs yesterday."

"Ah well, I'm thankful it's just theft. Things can always be replaced. I was apprehensive it might be something more sinister than that, like murder," expressed Datuk Seri, relieved.

Romy said quietly. "I'm afraid a murder has already been committed, Datuk Seri." He paused. "Rauf never went back to his hometown."

He saw the horror in his employer's eyes, which swiftly turned to an immense, unspeakable sorrow. It was painful to watch.

"Takziah, Datuk Seri." There was little else Romy could offer other than his condolences. "I saw your likeness in Rauf's photo. I'm correct, then, in deducing he was also your son?"

Datuk Seri Hasnul blew his nose on his vintage Aquascutum cotton handkerchief and made a monumental effort to pull himself together. "We do silly things, sometimes, PI Romy, as we grow older. Especially on turning 50. That's like a watershed year. Just to feel young once more or buang tabiat, maybe. But I did love Rauf's mother for a time. She was a gold star hostess in a dangdut lounge at Wilayah Complex. What was I thinking, a man in my position, frequenting such an establishment! Oh, how she could sing! 'Asyik, asyik, asyik / Asyik, asyiknya bercinta…'," crooned the Datuk Seri and sighed wistfully.

'Ku-ku-ku punya cinta'aa… / Ku-ku-ku punya rinduu…' Romy found himself almost taking up where Datuk Seri had left and warbling along. *Hell yeah.* Dangdut songs had this seductive effect on the senses. Very alluring. They could even be described as hypnotic. Something to do with the combination of sliding the palm on the tabla head to create a modulating sound and simultaneously plucking the mandolin strings.

Datuk Seri Hasnul hastily cleared his throat and got back to the point. "Rizz figured out soon after Rauf came to work for me, that Rauf is – was – their brother from another mother. He's very perceptive. That's why he's been exceptionally moody. I don't believe the others know. But still, to kill one's own brother! Such an evil, heartless crime!" lamented the Datuk Seri bitterly, more to himself. "I realize it means having to share the family fortune with Rauf, but each of my children will receive more than the average person can dream of having in several lifetimes. How much will ever be enough for Rizz?"

"No, Datuk Seri," Romy corrected him. "It wasn't Rizz. You mentioned Rauf had left a message with one of the others? About having to rush back to his hometown?"

"It was Jake who informed me," the Datuk Seri said slowly. "Jake!" he repeated. "Rauf must've confided in him who he was. They sometimes played those computer games together. And liked to dress up in samurai outfits. I thought it a bit strange but harmless enough. But I had always stated my intention of apportioning a decent sum of money for Jake in my hibah. I mean, five million isn't too measly, is it?"

The Datuk Seri's tone became contemptuous. "I see it now. Jake's – how do you say it, kiasu? – mentality. With Rauf coming into the picture, he viewed it as 'more men means less share'. And Jake is not even one of our own. He definitely does not have any right of inheritance under faraid. My sister and her husband adopted him when they couldn't have another child after Fenny."

He sighed again. "I realize now, too. My problem is I am too kind. Always assuming the good in human nature." A thought struck him. "My katana sword. Was that what Jake used..?"

His shoulders shaking as he was once more overcome by an inconsolable sorrow, Datuk Seri Hasnul suddenly seemed to have aged twenty years.

Romy gently put the broken handle he had found earlier on the Datuk Seri's desk. "Yes, the sword was the murder weapon. Jake must have enticed Rauf to go out on a walk with him. Reenact a mock sword fighting scene for fun. Cosplay, I think it's called. Then killed him."

Datuk Seri wept openly now. "Such is my fate. Not only to cry for my wife still living but to grieve for my son recently died."

Through the window, Romy could glimpse the arrival of a white Proton Wira, with the reassuring letters POLIS painted along its side.

It was for them to take over now. They would know best how to handle Jake. And to charge Fenny.

Perhaps, having too much money is overrated after all, he thought.

Aah, but if he could have his own helicopter… How cool would that be for Aiman!

Romy shook himself out of his reverie. *'Things.'*

7

✕

PI ROMY GOES BEHIND THE SCENES

✕

PI Romy took a cautious bite of his KyoChon crunchy chicken drumette.

He wasn't really an adventurous eater. But his recent assignment for a very atas Datuk Seri had introduced him to fine dining, so he now felt compelled to be more discerning in his food choices.

He had considered checking out the latest McD promotion tie-up with some famous pop group. There had been a lot of hype about it. But the queue had been absurdly long. Romy couldn't fathom why as it was essentially their usual nuggets and fries dressed up in a fancy paper bag. It was just a new choice of dips which made it different. Korean-inspired, apparently.

Hmm. He'd never tried Korean. He still liked his fast food fix, though. But he decided, maybe he should up the ante slightly above McD and KFC.

"We're actually not a fast food joint, Sir," the guy at the counter explained, when Romy asked why his order was taking a while. "We cook to order, so our food is fresh each time. We also use only chilled, antibiotic and hormone-free chicken. And we fry exclusively in premium canola oil, scientifically proven to be beneficial for health."

The guy continued to prattle on importantly, about their sauces being free from additives and going easy on their batter, so all their chicken pieces were tastier and less fatty than most other fried chicken establishments.

But it was information overload for Romy. He was damn hungry and just wanted his chicken.

He wasn't so sure it was worth the wait but ya, it tasted not bad. Delicious, actually. It would've been nice if he could have eaten at the restaurant itself, instead of in his car.

Damn Covid.

He sighed. How many more lockdowns would everyone have to endure in its name?

Romy was careful not to get any crumbs on the dashboard or seat of his new Ativa. Fastidiously, he doubled wiped his hands with wet tissues after he was done. It would never do to have grubby marks on the steering wheel.

Now to head home for his 2 pm 'call time'.

Wow, who would have thought, he mused, as he sped down Jalan Tun Razak toward Sentul. His debut on the silver screen. How cool was that!

Perhaps he'd request to be listed in the credits as ROMY ISHAK. That had a star quality vibe about it, *fuyohh, don't play-play*. And Ishak was, after all, the name of his paternal grandfather.

'We can only pay 800,' the producer, someone called Tay, had explained in an email. 'We're a tight outfit, just starting out. Hope it's okay.'

That was more than okay for Romy. He still harbored hopes of fulfilling his boyhood dream of becoming an actor.

Wait, he was getting ahead of himself, as usual.

First, he had to get through the audition. Online, of course.

Fortuitously, he had invested in a new computer not long ago, after his clerk had abruptly given her notice. The trending WFH had also made it pointless to carry on having an office space, and business wasn't exactly booming.

He clicked on the Google Meet link and waited for someone to let him in.

"Hiya, PI Romy, so glad you can join us today."

Romy hadn't bargained for six fresh young faces observing him intently from their individual panels on his computer screen. He'd thought it would just be the director and producer.

It was also his first time ever, attending a meeting online.

"Let me introduce our team," the voice went on.

Heck, which one of them was it, who was speaking, they were all sitting so darn still.

Oh, it was the dude in the top right corner.

Heikal, the film director. An enigmatic-looking young man with an unshaven face and a black t-shirt with the word OBEY scrawled across the front of it.

Romy went through the motions of nodding and smiling at each team member as Heikal made the introductions. His hand shook involuntarily as he tilted his screen to capture the best light.

Shit, it was dumb being nervous when he had no reason to be. They were merely a bunch of bourgie kids, recently graduated from some prestigious film school overseas. They had just returned home but first they had to undergo the obligatory 14-day quarantine at a hotel.

Romy wasn't sure which hotel. Had Tay mentioned it was the one on Yap Kwan Seng? Or perhaps it was Jalan Pinang. Somewhere in the KLCC area, anyway.

"Tay, our producer, who initiated contact with you via email…"

Romy took in the latter's short razored Mohawk haircut. Possibly how his son Aiman might describe as 'killin' it'. Romy always aspired to be a cool dad. He wondered if he might try the style the next time he went to the barber.

"Jin, our DOP –"

"DOP?"

"Oh, director of photography," Heikal explained. As if on cue, Jin held up his GoPro Max to the screen. His gender fluid wolf cut hairstyle was in sharp contrast to Tay's badass look and Heikal's moody stubble.

"Jenny, our make up & wardrobe supervisor…" Her cute black bucket hat bobbed merrily, as she flashed Romy a warm smile. It was infectious and she was so pretty, he couldn't help grinning inanely back at her.

"I wish I could offer you a Frappuccino, PI Romy," she said, holding up a pair of tall transparent cups, with the familiar logo of a mermaid with two tails on the side of each cup. "I only ordered one but they delivered two."

"You can drink the other one for me," Romy replied gallantly, still smiling foolishly at her.

"Ermm… PI Romy, if I may continue with the introductions," Heikal reminded him.

"Yes, of course." Romy regretfully fixed his gaze on the next panel.

"Sugananthan – Sugan – in charge of art & design."

"Big tings we inna, yo, Pea Eye?" Or perhaps he could have meant, "Pee? Aye!!" Sugan's velvety intonation, followed by a deep-throated chuckle, could have inferred either.

Cool dad aspirations aside, Romy wasn't sure about the rap genre of music. Most of the time, he hadn't the foggiest what the rapper was "sayin'."

"Like it were jus' a stream o' words comin outta hi' mout… dat wat yo mean, Pa?" Aiman had joked.

Nope. It was also the tone: it grated on Romy's ears as passive-aggressive and disrespectful.

Sugan had a disarming vibe about him, though, and none of those heavily tattooed biceps associated with rappers. Yet, fashion forward leaf-patterned pyjamas seemed inappropriate in the middle of the afternoon.

"Suzie – Sue – in charge of sound," Heikal rounded off the introductions and made a circular shape with his thumb and forefinger for all to see. "Okay, Team, good to roll!"

Surreptitiously, Romy clicked a few screen shots to share later with Aiman. His son would be so chuffed to see his Pa *otw to fame and stardom, uolls.*

Yup, Romy was well ahead of himself.

"Need to record the room tone… right, it's fine. We'll just get your voice warmed up, yes, PI Romy? Let's try a mic check."

Now, who the heck's that? Oh, Sue the sound machine. Romy wished it could have been Jenny instead.

"If you can answer a couple of questions for us." Sue consulted the blued-steel, diamond-shaped arrows of her Pasha de Cartier watch.

She was attractive but in a superficial way. Her double eyelids had likely been enhanced by a skilled surgeon, as had her contoured jawline. There was also a hoity-toity vibe in her manner, which reminded Romy of his ex-wife.

He felt his acting prospects immediately take a downturn.

"How tall are you, PI Romy?"

"Uhh, five eight."

"Weight?"

Romy lied about this one. "68 kg."

"Age?"

Another lie. "Uhh, 49."

"Marital status?"

"Available," he replied a little too loudly, with a devil-may-care laugh. Except unfortunately, in his zeal, he sounded like he was leering.

There was a discomfiting silence.

Sue played with the medallion on her Dior rose des vents necklace, languidly switching it between its moon and sun sides, before moving onto the next question. The better for all to ingest the impact of his utter embarrassment.

Romy decided then and there that he hated her.

"Occupation?" Sue finally decided to continue.

Heck, everyone already knew the answer. That was why he'd been contacted to try out for the role in the first place. "Private investigator."

The frame of Jin's panel lit up, indicating he was speaking. Romy was beginning to get the hang of how the process worked.

"PI Romy, if you can just move back a bit from the screen, so we may have a wide angle shot of you."

"You mean, like this?" Romy slid his chair away half a metre.

"Perfect."

"Oh, is that your cat we see in the background, PI Romy?" gushed Jenny.

Brad! Drat. "He's not actually my cat," he was about to elaborate. *Hell, did it matter?*

"So cute! Look, he's coming toward your computer." Jenny was ecstatic.

"So he can keep an eye on your mouse," quipped Tay, with a straight face.

Everyone except Romy chuckled.

"Okies, you got the script in front of you? We'll begin your audition now, PI Romy," Heikal decided, bringing everyone back to order. "Let's try the bibimbap scene at the café."

"Take it from the top, yea," Tay cued him. "Three, two, one. And... action!"

"Yo, yo, wait up! Are we doin' da scene about da bi-bim-bap?" interjected Sugan.

Sue groaned. "Duhh, Sugan."

"No need to get hissy, missy!" Sugan leaned forward to brush off a fleck on his screen monitor as he spoke. The glint in his eyes was evidence he hated Sue, too.

Tay cued Romy again. Romy didn't quite know where to focus his gaze and accidentally dropped the script onto the floor.

Brad pounced on one of the scattered pages, dug his paws into the paper, then jumped back up and sat himself firmly beside the keyboard, looking angelic.

Jin exclaimed, "Oops, catastrophe!"

Jenny giggled delightedly and clapped her hands, showing her Chanel pearlescent nude manicured nails to their best advantage.

Sugan started drumming a rhythm obstreperously with his pen on the buttons of his keyboard.

Tay tried to tell Sugan to, "stop that godawful drumming".

But Sugan had embarked on some unintelligible rap rhyme to match his drumming and couldn't hear him.

Sue rolled her eyes and resignedly twirled the cascading ash blonde tresses of her hair.

Romy gathered the scattered pages, shoving Brad off the table in the process, who yowled indignantly and hightailed it out of the room.

Finally, Heikal declared loudly above the racket. "Let's try this again, shall we."

"No need to shout!" snapped Sue, almost shouting herself.

Instantly, everyone's nerves perceptibly took a ragged turn. The present tiff was erupting into a shouting match.

Tay's voice was raised. "No one's shouting!"

"Yes, you are!" retorted Sue. "All you and Heikal have been doing every time we have a meeting, ever since we got back to KL is shout, shout, shout!"

"Heck, Sue. Thanks to you, actually it doesn't feel like we're back in KL," remarked Jin. "More like Kay Yell."

If this were a screenplay, at this point, the writer would scribble "BEAT" in the script, to indicate a shift in tone and propel the story forward to a new stage.

But the reality of the situation was seven people meeting virtually, via a Google app.

"We'll begin again, from the top." Heikal's tone was authoritative. He peered into the screen. "PI Romy?"

"Yes, yes," Romy took a deep breath and was about to utter his opening line, when there was the ring of a doorbell.

"Sorry, that must be Housekeeping with my clean sheets. Just a moment, guys," Tay apologized sheepishly.

There was an irritated groan from Sue. "For fark's sake, man, we'll still be doing this damn audition till dinner time. Tell them to come back later."

"He just has to pick up the sheets from outside his door. It won't take more than a sec. No biggie," countered Jin, coming to Tay's defense.

"But yeah, Sue has a point. We haven't even gotten started." Even gentle Jenny was beginning to sound frazzled.

"S'all good, guys, I'm back." There was a faux cheery tone in Tay's voice. "'Kay, PI Romy. All yours. From the top... three, two, one –"

There was the sound of a phone ringing.

"What the –" interpolated Heikal.

"Oh, s'ma phone," piped up Sugan coolly. "Hang in there, peeps, won't be long. Ah really need to take dis call, y'all."

"Goddamnit, Sugan!" yelled Sue. "You know the rules! It's phones OFF during auditions and rehearsals! You're so unprofessional, I swear. Probably looking to score some weed from your dealer."

"Woah, cool it, gurrl!" interjected Jin. "Sugan's cleaned hisself up."

"Yeah, tell da wurl 'bout ma druggie shiiit," said Sugan bitterly.

"I can sugar coat the deets if you want, loser!" taunted Sue.

But Sugan had turned off his camera to answer the call.

The sound of yet another doorbell was audible but it couldn't be ascertained as to whose door.

Sugan turned his camera back on. It had been a quick call indeed, as he'd said. He recommenced his drumming. This time, his words were clearly intelligible.

"Yo Sue / Ah know wat you do / Ah'm seein' red / Yo too well fed / So drop dead / On your head / On da bed / Drop dead / Drop dead –"

"Stop it, Sugan!" Jenny's voice was unexpectedly shrill with fear. "You're scaring me!"

"Where is Heikal?" Tay asked. "His screen is off."

Despite the virtual setting, with each ensconced in the security of their individual safe space, there was a strange atmosphere of unease, which seemed to extend beyond the screen. Like an evil hand enveloping them together in an invisible clasp.

Romy, too, felt it.

He looked round for the pesky but comforting presence of Brad as a reliable barometer of normalcy. But true to form, just when he was needed, the useless little fleabag had made himself scarce and disappeared.

"Where is Heikal?" Tay asked again.

There was a hollow 'poiing' sound as Heikal's screen came on and the outline of his face appeared close up on his panel. He had altered the position of his laptop so his image was against the light.

"I'm here," he responded tersely. "You were all pissing me off so I decided to take a leak."

Romy coughed discreetly.

"Sorry, PI Romy, I didn't mean you. But the rest can be a bunch of jerks, if left unchecked."

"Hoi, basket case, speak for yourself!" This was from Jin.

Sugan started again. "So Ah said / A to Zed / Vaccinate / Don't procrastinate / Or drop dead / Drop dead –"

"It's nobody's damn business if I choose not to take the vaccine!" Jin muttered.

"Sue's screen is on but she's not there," observed Romy, keeping his voice neutral.

"The doorbell!" Tay said. "It must've been Housekeeping bringing her fresh towels or something. Sue?" he called out inquiringly. "Suzie? Oh shit, can you please answer?"

"Maybe she's in the bathroom," Jenny said tentatively.

"Unlikely," Heikal said briskly. "Not at this time. She's very disciplined in her personal habits."

"Yeah, like my teachers before at school," chortled Tay. "I thought it was like they weren't human. Never once saw them enter the washroom."

"Trust you to be hanging round the toilets," sniggered Jin.

"Piss off, laddie... or should I say, Lady." Tay curled his lip. His mohawk which previously had looked quirky and on trend, suddenly made him look fierce and menacing.

"What's that?" asked Romy sharply. "On Sue's screen. Can you see?"

There was a shadowy figure in the background, who seemed to be walking unsteadily toward the front.

Jenny cried out, "Suzie babe!"

Sue staggered up to her screen.

With a sickening notion of dread, Romy saw blood oozing from the side of her head.

"Help," she whispered weakly. "I've been shot."

It was a pure reflex action on Romy's part to take a couple of screen shots.

Her outstretched hand flailed wildly, as if in an attempt to somehow climb through the screen, tilting the monitor at a sharp angle in the process. There was a soft thud as her head lolled to one side and she slumped onto her keyboard.

Weirdly, this seemed to give her the propulsion to bounce up feebly and take a few jerky steps backward, before landing in a half-sitting position against the pillows on the bed, like a horrible wallpaper image frozen on her screen.

Romy was the first to react. "Call Reception and tell them what happened. Don't leave your rooms."

Pandemonium immediately broke out. Everyone seemed to be scrambling for their in-room phone and yelling so loud and so hard, it was impossible to hear what they were saying, or even to see them clearly.

Only Jenny was sitting quite still in front of her screen. "I think there was something in this second cup of 'ccino. I don't feel – " She swayed and hit her face gracefully, right cheek first, against the table edge.

Romy instinctively jumped up and then sat down again. What could he do? He was miles away from the scene.

Heikal was peering so close into the screen, his features appeared distorted. "Shit, Jenny, you okay? Jenn?"

Sugan announced in a sepulchral tone, "She dead, man."

"No, likely just fainted lah. Delayed reaction, seeing Sue drop dead liddat," remarked Heikal, still attempting to keep the whole tragic situation on an even keel.

Jin rubbed his nose agitatedly. "This is crazy. Nobody's picking up the phone at Reception. And my door's locked. I can't get out of the room."

Tay said, "Shit. What do we do now?" He pounded his fist against his forehead in despair. "Oh wait, I think there's someone knocking on my door."

"Don't be so fast to open it. You don't know who –" warned Romy.

But Tay's figure could be seen rapidly going toward the door. The distant visuals were blurry and the voice from outside was inaudible.

It was obviously somebody known to him, as he remarked, "Thank God you're here."

Romy felt a momentary surge of relief. It was likely the hotel security. They would be able to handle the situation. "Tell them to get to Jenny as quickly as possible!" he called out.

Tay's screen appeared to be breaking up into wavy lines. And so was everyone else's.

Damn, what a time for the internet to be unstable. "Tay!" Romy called again.

It was about ten seconds before the connection stabilized.

There seemed to be a violent altercation going on at the far end of Tay's room. Romy strained to see who the other person was. It looked like a guy.

Tay was shouting, "What the freak, man! What the freak!"

Then, there was the glimmer of a pocket knife.

Romy recognized it immediately as a classic 112 Buck Ranger, with its iconic clip-point blade. He'd carried one around with him too, when he was in Bosnia. It had been useful for a lot of things, including quartering a chicken and gutting a fish.

He'd given the knife as a parting present to that little boy he'd rescued in Sarajevo. *No, not given.* It was pantang to gift someone with a sharp object. "You keep this for me till we meet again, Emir."

"Hvala, Leftenan Romy. Vidimo se."

Shit. Now was not the time to reminisce.

Tay and his mystery visitor were tussling for the knife. They inched nearer toward the screen.

Romy jammed his screen button to grab some shots.

But the maddening thing was that the other person – it was definitely a guy – whether by coincidence or design, kept his face totally away from the camera.

Not that he would have been instantly recognisable, as he was wearing a face shield as well as a surgical mask.

Suddenly, there was a blood-curdling, stomach-churning groan. Then, before Romy's horrified gaze, the unknown assailant was triumphantly brandishing what looked like Tay's digestive organs before the screen.

Holy shit, that was the liver, that was the colon, and the small intestine. Damnit, was the maniac now, actually juggling Tay's kidneys and gall bladder, the sick fuck. "Oi!!" yelled Romy. He jumped up from his chair and hurled obscenies at the computer monitor.

Meanwhile, Sugan had started his infuriating drumming again. "Yo, Tay / You want your way / Can, meh / But you gotta pay / Drop dead / Drop dead –"

"Shut up and do something!" roared Romy, shaking his screen in frustration.

Sugan held his hands up in midair and assumed a conciliatory tone. "Whoa! Eezeh, Uncle, no fightin' no fighting', I'm all guud!"

Romy took a deep breath and surveyed all the panels on the screen. The only other animate and hopefully sane person seemed to be Heikal.

Wait a minute, what about Jin? His camera was on but he was nowhere to be seen. Romy tried to speak as calmly as possible. "Did anyone see Jin leave his room?"

Heikal stroked his chin thoughtfully and seemed to be gazing in fascination at a point behind Romy's head.

Weirdo, there was nothing to see. Just his tattered Fella Design sofa set and one comfortable Lorenzo leather recliner, which had also seen better days.

"No, can't say I did," Heikal replied finally, still seemingly mesmerized by Romy's furniture.

The fellow was beginning to creep him out but Romy stubbornly refused to look behind him. There was really nothing there, okayyy.

Unless… maybe someone had entered unseen and was sitting quietly on the sofa.

Romy felt the hairs on the back of his neck stand on end. *This is ridiculous,* he reasoned to himself.

"Jin?" he called out casually into the screen.

To Romy's unspeakable horror, there were some horrible, lugubrious, gurgling noises emanating from the recesses of the screen. The image of Jin slowly emerged, with a bloodied forehead and a foaming mouth.

"This – this – monstrous giant-like – I dunno what… v-virus? It attacked me," he moaned weakly. "Please – help."

He head butted the screen, then collapsed.

Now this was deffo over the top.

A mindfuck of a dream, Romy told himself firmly. It just had to be. The long-buried nightmares of his active army service, manifesting themselves after a heavy lunch.

Those tiny pickled cold radish cubes had gone so well with the chicken, though. And indulging in a cold beer when he got home afterward, to calm his pre-audition nerves, had obviously been a bad idea.

Audition.

Shit, this was no goddamned dream.

It was a matter for the police.

Romy made a speedy mental checklist, as to whom among his police contacts he could call.

Heck, he couldn't think of any of them who wouldn't dismiss his garbled account jokingly with, "Pil kuda apa kau makan, 'My?" Followed by a suspicious, "Mana kau dapat?"

Pil kuda. Malay slang for meth. *Hah, if so, this would be the grandmother – no, the nenek kebayan – of all pil kuda.* It was a bloomin' nightmare.

"Yo Pea Eye / Oh my / Don't lie / You high? –"

The bugger had started on his stupid rap rhymes again. But. *Holy shit! Did this saphead also happen to be a bloody mind reader?*

Anyway, taking a step back, Romy reasoned, *none of these shitty events have anything to do with me.* Heck, he was just an innocent bystander.

"Cut that crap, okay!" he yelled angrily at Sugan. When Romy was agitated, he tended to bluster. "F-four murders! Four murders, I tell you! And all you can do is rap about it. I'm – I'm calling the police."

Heikal automatically seemed to come out of his reverie on hearing the word 'police'. "No, don't do that, PI Romy. It's not your call. Why get involved?"

Romy was completely baffled. "What The – ! Can I advise you SOMETHING?!! There's a bloody maniac on the loose. You both should be scared shitless. Unless…"

He looked at Heikal and then at Sugan. Not only did it not make sense, the sequence of events with them as the perps didn't add up.

Heikal smiled at him, a slow, secretive smile.

This time, Romy was totally creeped out. "Impossible," he muttered.

He was skeptical of the occult, with all its concomitant practices. Half-remembered childhood stories of restless ghouls, lurking by the pokok pisang behind his grandma's kitchen in Tampin, flitted through his mind.

Heikal continued to smile steadily at him.

For a few seconds, Romy was that close to peeing in his pants, he was totes petrified. That, if he turned round, he would find the bugger sitting in exactly the same position. On his sofa. And worst of all, still smiling.

Sugan, meanwhile, had plucked a couple of virulent green coconuts out of nowhere, one in each hand, and was rocking forward and backward, chanting in a strange dialect. It sounded like Kelantanese. Or perhaps Thai.

It was a virtual madhouse.

Romy swallowed nervously and willed himself to stay calm. Then, he remembered the screenshots he had surreptitiously taken earlier.

"Give me a minute," he said abruptly. He switched off his camera.

Ignoring Heikal's pleas of "PI Romy, please turn your camera on," Romy carefully studied each of the photos he had taken.

They were pretty horrific. Gruesome.

But the one of Sue, with a bullet through her head… That was strange, he didn't recall hearing any gunshot. Maybe the shooter had used a silencer.

He chewed his thumb thoughtfully, as he looked yet again at Sue's photo. Shot in the head with a bullet. Simultaneously, it triggered something which had been bothering him ever since her murder happened.

Of course. Why hadn't it occurred to him early on?

He waited for Heikal to ask urgently one more time, "PI Romy, can you switch back on your camera at once? Now, PI Romy. Please!"

Romy clicked the requisite button. Only Heikal's camera was still on. All the others had their cameras turned off.

"I should've straightaway realized," Romy told him, his words coming out in a rush. "When Sue got shot. A bullet hole through the head never looks neat. It blows the face away. And death would be instantaneous. No time to bob up and down like a ghost in a Chinese movie."

Everyone else's cameras immediately switched back on.

"Whoa, nothing escapes you, hey PI Romy," commented Heikal admiringly. "Well done for spotting that. But we had to film it that way. It's what our audiences would expect. If you don't mind, can we do another take, of what you just told me? And align your face more toward the center of the screen."

"Just a moment, let me adjust my lens," said Jin.

"Oh, also, if you can speak your lines more slowly, PI Romy," reminded Sue. "So it will be clear to our audience when they watch, how you came to solve the 'crimes'."

✕

That was an interesting experience, Romy thought to himself, as he did a quick sweep of his apartment for spooks.

He had to hand it to the team. They had made it all seem so real, he couldn't help still feeling a little unnerved.

According to Tay, once a technical process called the 'post' was done, the movie would be complete. There was even a mention of selling it to a satellite TV provider.

Romy could hardly contain his excitement at the possibility.

Meanwhile, it was already nearing his dinner time. Perhaps he would rustle up something simple in the kitchen. Probably just a Maggi asam laksa. Throw in a few chopped four-angled beans for some green crunchiness. Ah, but someday, when he got to be a famous movie star...

Ping went his phone.

It was a WhatsApp message from Tay.

800 banked in. Sending dinner by grab for job well done. Hope you like Korean. Crispy fried chicken & Ssambap.

k tq. What's Ssambap?

Tay's reply, accompanied by a smiley emoji was almost instantaneous.

It's a Wrap! ☺

8

✕

PI ROMY LISTENS WITH HIS EYES

✕

PI Romy was having chills. He'd taken four Panadols but they were still multiplying.

Damn Covid.

Truth be told, he was terrified of needles. But it was the only effective way to combat the virus, so the MKN messages on his handphone kept reminding him.

'Lakukan tanggungjawab dan jadi penerima vaksin. Lindung Diri, Lindung Semua!'

'Setiap jenis vaksin yang anda terima mampu membina perlindungan dalam badan untuk mengurangkan risiko ancaman Covid-19!'

'Vaksin yang akan diberikan telah melalui proses penilaian ketat.. yakinlah!'

Yada yada yada.

So he had dutifully registered and assumed his most blasé expression as he waited in line for his jab.

"Yes, there are side effects but usually temporary. Also, elderly people don't experience the effects so much," the young doctor guiding him through the pre-vaccination consultation patiently reassured Romy, in answer to his repetitive questioning.

Romy was approaching his 57th birthday so he felt duly senior enough to come within that category.

He felt fine for the first few hours afterward. Great, actually. Just a bit of soreness in his left arm where the needle had been. So much so, he contemplated doing a quick home workout using his Nike app.

But while he was selecting which session to do, all at once, an overwhelming fatigue hit him. The floor beneath was melting away, if that could be possible. As he found himself swaying, he could have sworn he was hearing violins.

He wished he hadn't gorged on that hearty teatime snack of apam balik gebu and teh botol earlier. It was all he could do to hold it in.

Shortly afterward, he found himself shivering like a lone shaved bird in a Sarajevo winter. Feeling precious and sorry for himself, Romy wrapped a blanket round his shoulders and ground his teeth to stop them from chattering.

Because he was so seldom ill, his current discomfiture was harder for him to endure. As a distraction, he turned on the TV to watch the news.

Bad idea. Cheerless, to say the least. Times were so hard for a lot of people.

There was a grim report on the increasing number of patients being brought in dead at hospitals, especially in KL and some of the larger towns. According to experts, it was likely due to an undetected Covid variant. So deadly, they were dropping like flies. Spanish flies, as the estimable Minister in charge might say.

At the same time, there were also unconfirmed reports that some of the brought in dead patients from the streets of KL had gunshot wounds on them.

Could there be a serial killer on the loose? *Hah, how these TV stations like to sensationalize everything*, Romy opined cynically to himself.

Anyone know a serial killer who's targeting anti-vaxxers?

Ya, Covid-19.

As suddenly as his chills had come, they were gone. Only to be replaced by a high fever. It didn't seem so implausible to fry an egg on his forehead.

He staggered up from the sofa to look for some ice cubes, almost tripping over Brad, who was napping peacefully on the carpet.

That bloody cat.

Crap. He'd forgotten to refill the ice cube tray in the freezer. In his delirium, fortunately, he didn't realize he was calling out for his ex-wife.

Toward dawn, he slowly broke out in a sweat and felt better. The next thing he knew, it was broad daylight and Brad was pawing his face, demanding brunch.

He himself was feeling ravenous. Maybe he'd order from that nasi kandar place on Jalan TAR, what was it called?

Hell, his memory.

What he could recall was that their ayam madu was the best: crunchy with just the right amount of stickiness on the outside, juicy and tender within.

Maybe he'd add on a kari telur ikan and a few pieces of okra, also remind them to ensure the nasi was banjir.

What the heck was the name of the shop? Perhaps they were on Grab.

Great, there was a nasi kandar shop on the list, which sounded vaguely like them.

It had to be either the ayam goreng or the kari telur ikan for the lauk, though. Going for both would be too indulgent.

His thumb hovered as to which of the two items to key into his order, when simultaneously his phone rang.

It was his nephew, Asyraf.

Shit. Something must've happened to Irfan for one of his sons to actually call. They had always, at most, just messaged. Then again, why was he being so paranoid? It was probably nothing.

Damn Covid.

"Oh it's because I happen to be at Sentul Raya, Pak 'My. Thought I'd drop by."

Romy grunted an okeh in a pseudo avuncular fashion. He resigned himself to chomping on a quick slice of bread and peanut butter to stave off his hunger pangs.

He wondered what it was his nephew wanted. He deffo could not cope with any family beef right now.

To Asyraf and his siblings, Romy was their cool uncle, who'd been in war-torn countries to protect the innocent and was woke laidat.

To their mother Shila though, he was just her shiftless brother-in-law who occasionally borrowed money from her husband and then never paid it back. But she'd felt sorry for the girl Romy finally married. A pretty thing with an off-duty model look about her. She had foreseen straightaway it wouldn't last. And of course, it hadn't. His Marie Claire income was no match for the girl's Ferragamo aspirations.

Asyraf was thinner than the last time Romy'd seen him. Which was a change, as so many people he knew were obviously comfort-eating their way through the lockdowns.

Old normal or new normal, Romy was never one for hand kissing when an elbow bump would do.

"Teaching my children to be kurang ajar," Shila had complained, but not in his presence.

"So! What brings you to my turf, boy?" asked Romy in a jolly voice.

Not quite a boy, anymore. His nephew was 24. A Psychology major from Inti University and the overthinker of the family.

Irfan's plebby childhood angst had likely instilled middle-class pretensions in all his children.

Romy, on the other hand, was always quick to remind his own son where they came from. "My father – your Atuk – was just a sessions court clerk, Aiman, and don't you forget it."

"I dunno, Pak 'My," Asyraf sighed. "It's all so weird."

"What's so weird?"

"Uhh, life. Everything."

"Ya," agreed Romy.

"And crazy."

"Yup, that too."

They sat on in companionable silence.

That was what Asyraf appreciated about his uncle. He didn't judge and was deep. Even now, Pak 'My had a contemplative expression, like he was seriously thinking about the pronouncements Asyraf had just made.

Actually, Romy was thinking wistfully that it would've been the kari telur ikan and not the ayam goreng.

It was several more minutes before Asyraf spoke. "Sometimes I feel we're all like a bunch of performing monkeys."

Romy raised his eyebrows. "We?"

"Yeah, us the rakyat. Being made to dance our whole lives through, to the tune of power-grabbing politicians."

"Da-a-amn," agreed Romy, in a tone suggesting Asyraf had nailed it.

Actually, his mind was still on the nasi kandar that should have been. So he completely missed that his nephew was on the brink of unburdening something which was obviously troubling him.

Changing his mind, Asyraf muttered abruptly. "I gotta run, Pak 'My, if I'm gonna make it in time for the soup kitchen."

"Soup kitchen?" Romy hadn't envisioned the situation was so bleak.

"I'm a volunteer," his nephew explained hastily. Again, he was about to say more, then decided against it.

But this time, his uncle was more percipient. "Tell me what your problem is, 'Syraf. Can't promise to help, but at least I can listen."

$$\times$$

As Romy had said, he could listen.

There hadn't been anything really to tell, on his nephew's part, which hadn't already been told by a million young people or more nationwide in the past year. The Covid shit had hit everyone hard. But the current bunch of **** (description hidden due to profanity) leaders who should be leading the country out of the quagmire were behaving, in urban slang, like 'George W Bush.'

"He was in your time, yeah, Pak 'My?"

"Yeah. That joker who accidentally ended up as POTUS."

'Sept 13 2001 Our number one priority is to find Osama bin Laden, yesiree and we ain't gonna rest till we find him.'

'March 13 2002 I dunno where bin Laden is. I don't care. It's not that important.'

Yup, he the one.

"And now they're saying we have our own equivalent, too," Asyraf remarked wryly.

April 15 2021 The government has no intention of imposing another nationwide movement control order.

May 10 2021 The whole of Malaysia will be placed under the Movement Control Order (MCO 3) from May 12.

Uh huh. Malaysia Boleh.

So the boy was disillusioned. And depressed. Who wouldn't be. What poor timing to be young and starting out.

Romy truly wanted to say something, anything, that wasn't a cliché. But heck, what else was there, other than going through the drill of encouraging his nephew to look on the bright side and accepting whatever crap he was going through?

"Because hey, 'Syraf, where you are right now isn't where you'll always be."

Which Romy used to think was rather lame. His army counselor had trotted out the phrase more times than he cared to count. But it had worked. Fighting off that overhanging cloud which seemed intent on permanently darkening each day. Willing himself not to fall through the trapdoor of desolation and despair.

Just the usual small steps. Getting out of his comfort zone, as his counselor advised. *Which was like going into the twilight zone*, he had murmured wryly to himself, remembering another of his favorite boyhood TV series.

That was how he'd stumbled upon a poetry-reading session at a bookstore on Telawi in Bangsar. Yup, A Poetry Reading Session. Romy, who only ever read just the newspapers, and mainly the sports pages at that. The last book he'd read had been under duress and that was an abridged version of *Animal Farm* in Form 3.

Now, there he was. Listening To Poetry.

But the girl reading a poem aloud had piqued his interest. She had such a soothing voice; *soft, gentle and low, an excellent thing in woman*, he thought. Unwittingly, Romy had just quoted Shakespeare. Truly a sign from heaven that he was smitten.

He asked her out for coffee afterward and was surprised when she accepted.

Even more astonished and gratified, when after a few months of being together, she agreed to marry him. Their age gap was fifteen years.

> *'Will there really be a "Morning"?*
> *Is there such a thing as "Day"?*
> *Could I see it from the mountains*
> *If I were as tall as they?'*

A decade later, she confessed that she had accepted his proposal because she was sorry for him, he had such sad eyes.

Looking back now, Romy realized he should've been worldly enough even then, to know that pity was a poor substitute for love. *And so one learns, as the world still turns*. Heck, he was becoming something of a poet too.

Carry on a while more and he might even search out and read that extract of a poem she'd scribbled dramatically on a sheet of paper before she'd left.

With their son, Aiman, the Ikea Hafslo sprung mattress with frame & headboard, Tefal bakeware set and Elba Professional Range Cooker, the last of which he still had had five installments left to pay.

His nephew now, though. There was a fatalistic attitude about his demeanor. That was not good. It was obvious he was harboring some dark secret.

His faint blushes hinted that it was a romantic liaison. Likely, some girl his tight-assed mother disapproved of.

The banging on the front door made him jump. It had to be Aunty Wong. She hadn't the patience for pressing the buzzer.

"Itu Kani!" Aunty Wong was shouting. She was hard of hearing and assumed everyone else was, too. "Itu Kani! Manyak hali tadak mali!"

Romy thought, *Seriously?* And who the hell was Kani?

But Aunty Wong, heck, she was also beginning to sound like a poet. Eventually, after a jumbled and at times unintelligible monologue, Romy was able to piece together the cause of the old lady's agitation.

Kani was a Dewan Bandaraya general worker. "Dia sapu itu tepi jalan. Malam kerja."

Romy wondered idly how the fella was able to sweep at night. The streets were so poorly lit.

But it gave him time in the day to run errands for Aunty Wong, fix appliances and other stuff in her apartment. Surely Romy had seen him sometimes.

Hmm... ya, maybe. He vaguely recalled a small, swarthy fellow with a toolkit, waiting for the lift or darting along the corridor, carrying groceries. "Rupanya gelap-gelap sikit, kan? Macam Bangla atau Rohingya –"

Aunty Wong gifted Romy with one of her hard stares. "Dia Sentul punya budak. Latuk, bapak lia lulu suma kerja lelwei. Luluk itu kuaters depan pasar Sentul."

"Ohh. Orang kita. Sori, sori."

Getting back to Aunty Wong's narrative. To make a short story shorter, Kani hadn't been round to Aunty Wong's in several days. Nor had he called her to say he wasn't coming.

Apparently this was unheard of.

Plus, she owed him 30 bucks for helping to unclog the rings of her gas cooker. There was no way he would've missed coming by to collect his lui.

"Lomy misti cali dia," she instructed Romy imperatively.

Heck, how was he going to do that?

"Lu mata-mata, lu misti tau macam mana cali," she declared. "Sekalang jugak."

Futtocks. She reminded him of his mother.

$$\times$$

Romy could never fathom why Balai Polis Jalan Tun Razak had to be designed in such a way that its entrance was on Jalan Ampang.

Be that as it was, it was his 'go to' police station. The reason was simple. He had friends there. And as far as police stations went, there was a reassuringly almost homely feel about it.

Despite Aunty Wong's reluctance, Romy had insisted that he lodge a missing person's report.

The Inspector friend he was hoping to meet with was out, but had left word with his Sergeant to attend to Romy. Courteously, the Sergeant took down Kani's details.

Prior to coming to the station, Romy himself had also done a quick sweep on the relevant portals for unidentified vics at the morgues in the past few days, none of whom matched Kani's description.

Romy knew that the Sergeant, on the orders of his superior, was graciously indulging him. The police force was over-stretched as it was, with all the Covid shit going on.

The desperation of the common folk was also taking its toll. It was super tough, especially for the women, who were more vulnerable. But more than a year on, the relevant minister's solution to that appeared to have progressed little, beyond advising wives to giggle coyly and address their husbands in their sweetest Doraemon voice.

Oh, and popping round from time to time to distribute food baskets to the disadvantaged, like a cosmetically enhanced, svelte Red Riding Hood.

He was signing the police report when a voice over his shoulder hailed him, "PI Romy?"

"Uhh... er... oh... Encik Sam!" Bother these masks. Such a job sussing out whom from who.

For the umpteenth time, Romy marvelled at how small KL was.

Take, for instance – when was it? – three months ago, maybe.

There he was, tucking into a plate of nasi goreng Hainan at Chee Meng on Bukit Bintang when, of all the chicken rice joints in all the towns in all the world, Najib and his posse had to walk into this one.

Anyway, that was unrelated to the present.

Sam Hasnul. That was a wretched little business with his cousin.

It appeared to be that, on bumping into Romy, Sam had second thoughts as to coming to see the police. "S'okay, Sargeant. I've decided not to make a report."

He followed Romy out of the building, nonchalantly whistling a few bars of a tune. Like he hadn't a care in the world.

"I say, PI Romy, can we talk? My pad's a couple of minutes' walk from here."

"'Kay, can."

Sam's "pad" turned out to be the penthouse suite of My Habitat, a sedate serviced residence, just a hop, skip and jump away from the police station. It had its own rooftop pool and hot tub, and an impressive open air home theater with a retractable awning, in case of rain.

Romy admired the view of Genting Highlands in the distance before going back indoors and accepting an ice cold Malta in a can.

"So how've you been, PI Romy?"

"Me? Okay, I guess."

"And the family? I mean, you have a wife? Kids?"

Romy never liked discussing his personal life with his clients. Least of all, divulging his failed marriage. He was private laidat. "Uh, I'm sure you didn't invite me round to ask about my family, Encik Sam," he laughed lightly, glancing round the well-appointed living room.

Its generously proportioned modular sofa set had obviously been designed and produced in an atelier in Firenze. Above it hung an original symbolist painting by the artist Edvard Munch. There was an abundance of bespoke framed photographs, interspersed amongst the array of books crammed on the shelves. It appeared evident that Sam was extremely well-read and had plenty of friends.

"You're darn right, PI Romy, I didn't." He pinched his forehead and said tiredly, "It's like this. You've heard of my family's charitable foundation, I'm sure."

Actually, Romy wasn't sure. "Hunger Hurts?" he hazarded a guess. "No, that's the youth one. Hope 4 Humankind, izzit?"

Sam nodded. "We work with the economically and socially marginalized groups. Refugees. People living with AIDS. The transgender community. Our mission is to protect those most at risk in our society."

"Uh huh."

"We've been making inroads, PI Romy. Slowly addressing the public's misconceptions and working toward achieving acceptance for those who may not conform to the criteria of so-called normal society."

"Uh huh."

"In fact, we recently…" Sam droned on.

Romy successfully stifled a yawn. *Could the fella just get to the point, pleazzze… so longwinded, just like his father.*

It was a relief when he finally did.

"I've been getting these threats, PI Romy. Normally, I don't give 'em much thought, there're a lot of crazy keyboard zealots around. But I seem to have cheated death three times in just as many days. It can't be a coincidence."

"Why didn't you want to tell the police just now?"

Sam hesitated and reset the checkers on the Ralph Lauren handcrafted backgammon board, which lay open on the side table next to him.

"Running into you made me change my mind. If anyone is to help me, it can only be you. You'd understand." He went on to utter the magic words, "Tell me your rates, PI Romy. I'll do an online transfer now."

As it happened to be the weekend, Romy's rates were double.

And as expected, Sam thought nothing of it. It was barely half the amount he spent on a night out at Marini's with a dozen friends.

Now that Romy's account was quite flushed, suddenly he was up for some small talk. "So, you were in the Middle East for a time, Encik Sam?"

"You noticed my photos. Yeah. Our Foundation does relief work in Palestine. I volunteered at the hospital in Ramallah. And I was also for a while in Bureij." Sam avoided Romy's eyes. "Astrid helped out there too. She drove an ambulance, ferrying sick kids. That's how she hurt her back. She took a hit from a lone IDF soldier. It was unintentional, he was a rookie, poor sod."

Romy marveled at Sam's magnanimity. He wondered if Astrid felt the same. Or indeed, if she had any feelings at all about anything.

He changed the subject and got down to business.

"'Kay, tell me about the attempts on your life these last three days."

$$\times$$

The bad news was that, there was no doubt that Sam's life was in danger.

The good news was that, the perp was almost certainly someone at the Foundation. This narrowed down the list of suspects considerably.

Romy arranged to come by the Foundation's headquarters at 6 pm.

"I'll introduce you as, erm… our new project advisor, PI Romy," Sam decided. "You can join our meeting and then be part of our group when we go on our alleyway cruise."

Donning a faded Puma England Euro 2016 jersey and his oldest pair of jeans, Romy decided to Grab it to the H4H office on the fringes of Kampung Baru, bordering Chow Kit.

The roads in the area were generally narrow. And he wasn't sure what time he would be done. He certainly wasn't going to risk parking his precious Ativa where there might be a risk of it getting scratched. Some people were just jealous for no reason.

The rebarbative Brutalist edifice which housed Hope for Humankind struck a discordant note among the graceful vestiges of century-old traditional wooden houses in its midst.

"We bought the building because it was abandoned during construction and going cheap," explained Sam. It was obvious he didn't want to be associated with such unloveliness, more than necessary.

The meeting was in a large room on one of the higher floors, looking onto the monorail leading toward Medan Tuanku station.

Similarly as in Sam's pad, photographs abounded. This time though, they were pinned on large soft boards on the wall.

Romy's keen eye took in several of the subjects in the photos. Not a single one of a politician. Instead they comprised mainly volunteers, a sprinkling of celebrities (*da-a-amn, was that Ed Sheeran?*), a few Royal personages, as well as visiting personnel from other humanitarian organizations.

There were eight people at the meeting including Sam and Romy, each well spaced out along the long table meant for twenty. Air coolers at each end of the room were infused with sanitizer spray, so everyone felt at ease enough to lay down their masks.

Astrid and Rizz were also at the meeting. Astrid was dressed down as usual, in pink sweats and an oversized hoodie. Rizz sported a vintage J.Crew v-necked tee and frayed black Dickies cargoes.

Romy didn't know how they pulled it off. The more casually they dressed, the wealthier they looked. It was an old-money thing.

If Rizz and Astrid were surprised to see Romy at the meeting, they showed no sign.

Sam's killer had to be one of the other four suspects, Romy was quite certain of that.

There was the Secretary, Chiew, feverishly transcribing the minutes throughout. It was evident he was completely familiar with them all by hearing, as not once did he look up from his tablet.

Then there was the Accountant, Johan, a shy bespectacled young man who was obviously in awe of Astrid and in love with Sam.

And Ashok, the General Manager. A confident, articulate man in his early forties, could he be capable of murder?

He remarked jokingly to Romy, "England won't stand a chance against Germany in the semis next week in this Euro cup, Uncle. I think the last time they won any major soccer tournament was when you were twelve years old."

"I was two, actually," Romy grinned. "Ya Ash, my memory is like an elephant's."

Finally there was the PR person, Cindy, with a sweet demeanor and the faintest trace of an American accent. The effect of growing up on a diet of *Pretty Little Liars* and *Gossip Girl*.

It was obvious she was new to the hijab, as her hair kept slipping out from beneath her fuchsia Soonaru x Sleepy Studio light crepe scarf.

Romy tried but could not, in honesty, imagine any of them in the role of murderer.

They were all collectively awash with altruism and genuinely passionate about their work. There was a clique-ish vibe, Aunty Wong would have described it as kam cheng.

Sam proved to be an adept chairman, allowing opposing views to be heard equally and summarizing the issues resolved, before moving on to the next item on the agenda.

Finally Chiew intoned quietly, his only verbal contribution to the meeting. "Sudah masuk waktu Maghrib."

The meeting was declared adjourned.

To Romy's surprise, he saw Sam had a nervous tic in his eye. Tiny beads of sweat were also visible on his forehead. The guy was bricking himself. Hmm, so Sam was one of those when it came to chairing meetings. Like a duck. Looking calm and chill on the surface, but under the water kicking like hell, trying to stay afloat.

During the short khutbah by Chiew, who had also performed the duty of imam for the congregational Maghrib prayer, Romy's thoughts strayed briefly to Sam's account of the recent attempts on his life.

The first time was mid-morning. The office makcik had made him his cup of sencha at 10.30, as she normally did. He'd had a couple of sips and it tasted fine.

Then suddenly, there was a small commotion at the reception counter. So he'd gone to check.

It turned out to be a young man who'd been asked to show his MyKad during a random check by the authorities. The officer had insisted his MyKad was likely a forgery, and bundled him into a truck with about fifty others. Somehow, along the way to the Immigration detention depot in Semenyih, the fellow had managed to flee from the truck, cracking his ribs in the process.

After some days in hiding and sleeping rough, he'd found his way to the H4H office and was begging for their help.

"I was away from my desk for only a few minutes," said Sam. "But when I drank my tea again, it tasted like someone had added an artificial sweetener, either Aspartame or Stevia. I couldn't drink it anymore. Erm… you know the antifreeze stuff they use in engine coolants – ethylene glycol – it's poisonous a.f. Has a killer effect on the kidneys. The thing is, it also tastes sweet. Later, I heard one of the drivers complaining that he couldn't find the canister of coolant he needed for the van radiator."

The second time was in the evening. Sam and Johan were having an audit meeting with their UK collab on Zoom.

"It had to be at night because of the time difference. There was some discrepancy about the figures which Johan needed to highlight, as the original file had gotten corrupted. So a couple of balances didn't tally."

Longwinded as usual. Just get to the point, man.

The meeting had ended very late. Sam was about to get into his car when he heard a loud bang. He'd brushed it off as a motorcycle backfiring.

Then he noticed a bullet casing on the ground, beside where he was standing.

"Do you still have it?" asked Romy.

"No, I panicked and quickly got in the car and drove off. I know I shouldn't have. I mean, I always carry my CZ." He patted the stolid outline at his side reassuringly.

"And just this afternoon, I'd entered the lift to go up to my pad. The doors were closing when this guy came rushing and tried to prise the doors to keep them open." Sam shivered involuntarily. "He was pointing a gun at me. I stopped the lift

three floors up. Then I took the emergency stairs down again and
fled out the back entrance and went to the police station. That's
when I met you. The point is, the guy was wearing an H4H polo
shirt. I'd know the logo anywhere. It's on the left pocket."

The khutbah was over. One of the staff hurried purposefully
toward Sam, with a sheaf of papers under his arm and his Galaxy
S21 Ultra in his other hand.

"Encik Sam, lucky I managed to catch you. These documents
urgently require your signature."

"Uh okay, but you startled me, Ilham," complained Sam.
"And why d'you have to carry such a big ass phone."

It was obvious the recent incidents were getting to him. To
Romy, he said, "Get a quick bite to eat from the canteen. We'll set
off on our cruise soon."

The canteen was abuzz with a long line of the disadvantaged
and marginalized, queuing to collect their bento box and bottle of
water.

Astrid handed one of each to Romy and said, "We can eat at
my desk."

Romy gingerly lifted the box flap. To his surprise, an appetizing
whiff of buttered rice and grilled filet o' fish filled the air. In one
of the other compartments was a freshly tossed salad and there was
also a slice of date cake, still warm from the oven in another.

Astrid saw his expression. "Nobody should have to suffer the
indignity of being fed scraps," she remarked. "And shame on those
who make a meal of feeding the poor, yet refuse to eat the same
food. Because it's not good enough for them."

Romy nodded agreement as he dipped a chunk of tenggiri into
the sos sambal asam provided. This tasted so good. He wondered if
there might be an extra box he could tapau for later.

"Leaving in ten minutes. Let's do the Alor circuit, for a change. We'll take the Nissan Vanette," Sam called out as he passed Astrid's desk.

Romy was slightly disappointed. He was thinking, surely the Hasnul children would want to ride in something grander. A Toyota Vellfire or Alphard, at least. *Why the heck do these turun temurun atas people have to be so double confirm weird laidat.*

Rizz, like Sam, had also chowed down with the other volunteers, an enthusiastic bunch of mostly younger people, vociferous in their views on tackling social issues.

"Dinner okay, PI Romy?" he murmured, as he walked by without expecting an answer. It was just one of those nugatory asides, courteously uttered in passing.

But he was a completely different person from that churlish young man Romy had met in Cameron Highlands not so long ago. His eyes crinkled engagingly as he spontaneously put an arm around one of the volunteers and chortled unrestrainedly at a joke. Their heads were bent closely together.

Then the couple suddenly realized they were being observed. Romy hastily looked away.

The drive to Bukit Bintang was smooth, with Astrid at the wheel. Ashok, Chiew, Johan and Cindy followed suit in Chiew's Honda Accord.

Once, they encountered a road block. But on inspection of their permit, the police coterie waved them through.

The momentary encounter with the policemen rattled Sam. "What the frick –" he could barely contain his irritation. "Like they have nothing better to do."

"Lighten up, bro. It's all good," Rizz, who was riding shotgun, reassured him.

Astrid parked the van expertly in a tight space on Jalan Bulan. Chiew drove on further ahead round the corner, where there was more room to steer.

They were familiar with the drill. Travelling in pairs, one carried a large thermal storage bag packed with bento boxes, while the other lugged a carton of plastic bottles of water.

Romy went with Sam, Astrid with Rizz, Ashok with Cindy and Johan with Chiew.

It was a fine, dry night. The sky was illuminated with a large bright moon, nicknamed a strawberry moon, the last of the supermoons for the year, when the moon was at its closest to Earth.

It was almost dystopian, what Covid had done. The stalls were all shut down. No more joie de makan.

Only a zigzag of tattered red lanterns strung from the colonnade of trees remained, as a reminder of the food porn which had seduced tourists and locals alike and kept them coming for more.

The group stepped softly as they wended their way along the grimy pavements. The volatility which was common in such situations made them extra vigilant when approaching their intended recipients.

> *I, being poor, have only my dreams;*
> *I have spread my dreams under your feet;*
> *Tread softly because you tread on my dreams.*

Some were in gregarious spirits, game for a bit of banter as they lolled about on their flattened cardboard boxes, their worldly possessions bundled together in a single canvas holdall or carefully stored in an assortment of plastic bags.

Others glared suspiciously but accepted the food placed for them with a surly nod. Romy had a grudging respect for those. It proved they still retained some semblance of pride.

Several appeared to be asleep, in which case the meal was placed a short distance away from them. It wouldn't do to wake them. They might be shocked into thinking they were being attacked and lash out in fear, with a weapon concealed about their person.

Sam craned his head in the direction of a grubby stairwell across the street. "Shhh… did you hear that?"

Romy hadn't heard anything.

"That rustling noise. And those shadows." Sam's voice was quavering.

"It's nothing. Just rats. Look, there's one jumping about, over there."

But Sam's disquiet was beginning to creep out Romy too.

The dimly-lit pavement threw up mysterious silhouettes on the mottled walls of the abandoned shopfronts. Cavernous black holes, where metal shuttered doors had been, seemed to beckon the unwary into their nether depths.

It was all becoming kinda spooky. Romy found himself inexplicably drawn toward the row of empty buildings, as if their ghostly inhabitants were reeling him in.

He breathed in sharply. *Get a grip, A271057H*. Romy quoting his army registration no. to himself was a manifestation of his ragged nerves. He checked the carton he was carrying. Just a bottle left, which meant one last meal to give out.

But now, damnit, where was Sam? Romy had turned his back only for a second and the bloke was gone. Vanished.

He felt a tap on his shoulder. "Sam! There you are. We still have one more –"

In the same instant, there was a God Almighty deafening report.

Rizz and Astrid came tearing down from the other end of the street.

"I got him, Sis!" yelled Sam triumphantly.

There were low groans of pain from the alleyway. Instinctively, everyone raced across to see who it was.

"You idiot! That's Chiew!" snapped Astrid angrily.

Johan was folding his thermal bag in half for a pillow to place under Chiew's head. "I think the shot just missed his lung, thank God."

"I'll bring the car round." The previously confident Ashok fumbled in Chiew's blood-drenched trouser pockets for the keys. "Fuckkit, where are they?" His hands shook.

"Go fetch the van." Astrid threw the keys at him. She cradled Chiew in her lap. Her eyes glistened with tears. "Stay with us, Chiew. Mengucap."

Romy swiftly leaned hard on the wound with his knee, exerting as much pressure as he could so the blood would clot.

But the blood continued to ooze out.

Rizz produced a stray piece of plastic wrap from his backpack, twisted it into a ball and attempted to seal the hole caused by the bullet.

Meanwhile, Cindy pulled off her tudung and tore it into strips to make a tourniquet.

Between them, Rizz and Johan propped Chiew up and proceeded to half-carry, half-drag him to the side of the road where Ashok had driven up with the van.

"I'm so very sorry." Sam was shaking like a leaf. "But you saw, right?" he whimpered to Romy. "He crept up on me. It's Chiew. He – he was trying to kill me."

Now, with the benefit of hindsight, Romy had indeed seen. And understood. How could he have not seen earlier?

$$\times$$

"It didn't kick off immediately," Astrid related to Romy as they hung around outside the hospital entrance, waiting for the doctor to come out and give his prognosis on Chiew. "Sam was fine for the first few months after our last sojourn in Gaza. Then, out of the blue, he became very jumpy, started having frightful nightmares."

Rizz took up the story. "Kept telling me privately that Astrid's injury was all his fault."

"But it went away and he was okay again for a long while," Astrid chipped in. "PI Romy, you were with us last month. Sam was pretty normal, right?"

"Yes," Romy agreed. "But then recently, it must have come back. His delusions. Sam was suffering from PTSD, am I right? Which made him believe he was being hounded. That someone wanted to kill him."

The shades came down again on Rizz's face. He was back to Cameron Highlands mode.

"The murders of those homeless people," Romy went on. "That was Sam, wasn't it? However hard he tried, he couldn't feel safe. He was having flashbacks of his ordeal in Palestine."

The shades came down on Astrid, Johan, Ashok and Cindy too.

"You can't prove it," they chorused defensively at the same time.

"When the bullet lodged in Chiew's ribs is removed and submitted to Forensics, I can."

There was a silence. They looked uneasily at one another.

Rizz's eyes narrowed. He seemed to be able to read Romy's mind.

Finally he said, "Yes, PI Romy, I know you can. But I also know you won't."

✕

It was nearly 3 am by the time Romy rolled into bed. Alhamdulillah, Chiew was ultimately going to be fine. InsyaAllah.

He was dead tired. But chasing sleep simply saw it slip further away.

How had Rizz known? It was true his father, Datuk Seri Hasnul, had described him as perceptive. Still…

"Is it so clearly written on my face?"

Romy prided himself in having put all that shit, as he termed it, well behind him. *There is no glory in war, only exploitation*, his army buddy Philip had lamented bitterly, after they had received their discharge, honorable though it had been.

In Romy's view, in the end, a war was never about who was right. It was about who was left.

He recalled trying to explain his nightly terrors to his then new wife, who couldn't possibly have been expected to understand. Her definition of bad dreams was limited to, "Oh my god, 'My, you know those shoes I like, which are going to be on sale? I dreamt they didn't have them in my size!"

So, all he could do was continue to take his medication, try to forget, just get the hell through the day.

And listen as his wife's dulcet tones, once music to his ears, began to grate on him, akin to the sensation of a dentist's drill probing a particularly sensitive tooth.

It was a relief when she asked him for a divorce.

Now that he thought about it, several years on, he'd never read what it was she'd written on that sheet of paper. Part of a poem, wasn't it.

Well, he couldn't sleep, and he was out of Melatonin.

Who knew? Perhaps reading it would send him straight off.

Except he couldn't for the life of him remember where he'd kept the paper. Hopefully he hadn't thrown it away.

He rummaged about for a bit.

Here it was. Right at the back of the drawer, where he kept his socks.

Oh, he hadn't realized. She'd actually copied out the whole poem. 'Remains' by Simon Armitage.

Romy read it through slowly several times before he got it. And then it resonated with him.

Heck. So his ex-wife had been more intuitive than he'd given her credit for. Oftentimes, the words never spoken speak the loudest.

He slept soundly after that.

$$\times$$

That goddamned banging again, fit to wake the dead.

Aunty Wong with her update. "Lomy, Lomy! Itu Kani sudah latang mali! Lia kena tangkap lor, bikin lia manyak susah. Tapi ada itu Yayasan punya olang kasi tolong sama lia."

So that was cleared up, whoopee! Now, please could he go back to sleep?

Oops, not yet.

His phone was ringing.

It was Asyraf. "Pak 'My, you saw me last night at H4H, yes?"

"Uh huh."

"So now you know."

"Uh huh."

"I never willed it to happen, Pak 'My. Much as I try, I just cannot feel the same way toward a girl. And it's the same with Rizz, too. He loves me, Pak 'My. Even when I'm at my worst."

"Uh huh."

"Maybe I can try explain it all to Ibu."

Romy was suddenly wide awake.

"No," Romy advised his nephew. "No, no, 'Syraf, don't confide in your mother. Tell your father instead. Believe me. He'll understand."

9

×

PI ROMY & THE ROAD LESS TAKEN

×

PI Romy awoke on his 57th birthday feeling very pleased with himself. He stretched his biceps exaggeratedly and nodded approvingly into the mirror.

"Not to brag," he murmured modestly to Brad, who was fastidiously sharpening his claws on the barbell rack by the window, "but I think I can give Zul Ariffin a run for his money."

All that pounding of the pavements in his Asics. And passing up on the second packet of nasi lemak and third kopi peng at the mamak. Yup, he'd got the payoff he wanted.

He wondered how he might treat himself to celebrate his special day. If it weren't for the current stupid MCO, he could've planned a trip somewhere with Aiman.

He missed his son.

Romy hated to admit it but ya, okeh lah, he was too indulgent a father. The boy was better off staying with the mother. And with school being online because of Covid, it was likely that Romy would just let him play Minecraft or Counter-Strike all day. Then if his ex-wife asked, complain that the WiFi connection was so slow, their son wasn't able to log in to class.

But where would they go, though, if they could travel interstate?

Hmm. Jeriau waterfall was a possibility, except it broke his heart each time driving through Fraser town. Insensitive urbanization was practically murdering the hill.

Maybe a hike up Gunung Datuk again. There was a pleasant Airbnb at Rembau that they liked. Nothing fancy but the makcik who owned it cooked a mean asam pedas ikan pari with buah keluak. Just the mention of the dish made Romy's mouth water. Buah keluak. In Romy's opinion, it was deffo Malaysia's underrated answer to France's truffles.

Fuyohh, his knowledge of gastronomy was expanding. So long as his waistline wasn't in tandem. Zul Ariffin. Huhuhu.

Pity about his birthday jaunt, though. Suddenly, he had a bucket list of destinations.

Faark. It was a no-choice situation. He'd just have to settle for a run round the Bukit Tunku circuit. He always enjoyed his sorties there, anyway.

Interspersed with the uber mansions of the ballin were smidgens of dense and lush wilderness, the last bastion of junglehood in the city. Because fortuitously, the terrain was too steep and economically unviable to elicit any interest from developers. When the mood took him, Romy had sometimes clambered down from the curb of Jalan Tunku, into what his ex-wife had previously lightheartedly referred to as 'the road less taken'.

That had been during those early, heady days of their courtship.

There was a hidden trail which wound steeply through the undergrowth and occasionally petered out. Eventually, it led to a tiny spring. Crystal-clear water tumbled several metres down an elongated, jagged slab of bedrock. It was so pristine and serene, it was possible that it was known only to himself. Romy had never met a soul in his forays in the area. And his then fiancée had been initially enraptured by it, too.

But the novelty had soon worn off. She preferred hanging out at KLCC or Mid Valley. There was nothing to see in the jungle. The same reason why Romy had no patience with going to shopping centers. "When you see one, you've seen them all," he'd remarked.

And he couldn't get why she'd chortled and repeated, "Seen them all… the mall. Get it?"

Get what?

Yup, the road less taken it was for him today.

He loved messing about in the jungle. The thick wad of wet leaves on the ground emitting a swooshing sound, despite his light tread. The slivers of sunshine creeping through the canopy of leaves overhead. Squeezing past a curtain of rough vines, as the sweat ran down the back of his neck. And all along the way, the buzzing and the humming and the chirping and the thrumming of the insect and bird jungle ensemble.

Occasionally, the piercing shriek of an indignant monkey would startle him out of his thoughts. But at the same time, it was somehow reassuring.

He ran lightly down the stairs, ten floors, from his apartment and then one more floor to the basement carpark. It was his usual light warmup.

A tune hummed in his head. It was one of those retro hits his battle buddy, AP, used to bellow incessantly in the barracks. There was a laidback vibe about it, which for some reason had kept their spirits high.

As he deftly maneuvered his Ativa out of its parking bay and up the ramp onto the main road, he racked his brain to remember the lyrics, then realized that except for the line about riding in a car and having the radio on, there was nothing else he could remember of the song. Not even the title, nor who sang it.

The original was by some dude, that much he could recall. But there was a sexy female version, which he preferred. Now, what was her name? No, maybe it was an all-girl group.

Romy hated it when his memory failed him. It was a sobering reminder of the onset of old age. It made him feel as if 57 was the new 75. *Sheesh, depressing, man.*

No matter. The song title might come back to him later. Or he could text AP.

He drove leisurely along Jalan Segambut with its car workshops and dilapidated warehouses, up the roundabout, turning at 11 o'clock onto what he still called Jalan Duta. Then it was a slight left into Langgak Tunku.

There was a café there that he liked, nestled in one of the shop lots on Taman Tunku. Perhaps he might pick up a coffee and pastry of some kind. They brewed excellent coffees each morning and baked fresh everyday.

A cortado, he decided, and a brioche au raisin swirl.

Fuyyohh. It was the consequence of rubbing shoulders with the have-haves that was giving him airs. I say… Next, he'd be insisting that his bottled water be San Pellegrino instead of Seamaster.

As he was ruminating at how atas he was becoming, he almost knocked over someone who was running zigzag on the road.

Silly bugger. Or perhaps he was fed up with life, not to look where he was going. Romy didn't really blame him. The Covid was playing ass with everyone's lives.

Damnit though, had he hit the fellow? Because the hapless sod had taken a tumble.

Romy stormed out of his Ativa and addressed the blaggard in Her Majesty's English. "You bloody fool! What the blazes!"

His ex-wife would've been proud.

Then again, I say, chaps, the original name of Bukit Tunku was Kenny Hills. The bourgiest 'hood in KL.

"Astarghfirullah, bukan sengaja, Boss." The pint-sized but wiry guy was groaning and rubbing his shin. He looked up at Romy with a dazed expression, before his dusky features immediately broke into a wide toothy smile of recognition.

"PI Romy! Boss! You tak ingat sama saya?"

Romy didn't know him from Adam. "Huh?"

"Kan dulu, Boss ada mari saya Mem punya rumah bila dia hilang itu barang kemas." He removed his mask momentarily (the better for Romy to see him, dear reader).

Y-y-ya, possibly. It was quite a few years ago. The case of a parsimonious tai tai who'd misplaced her pearls and tried to stick the blame on someone in her family. All the household staff had also been lined up for questioning as a matter of routine, and this chappie had obviously been one of them.

Exquisite and rare though the pearls had been, when they were finally found in her olive wood box, entangled with her rosary beads, what had stuck irrelevantly in Romy's mind was the house. It was huge. No, ginormous. And darned ugly.

"Ini saya rushing mau report polis. Itu Mem tadak keluar bilik. Cuba ketuk ketuk, dia tak jawab. Bilik kunci."

What the freak, the bumbling pushover was expected to ankle it nearly 5 km to the nearest police station, which was Sentul. *These people don't have car or what.*

Romy's upper-crust pretensions, like his chances of grabbing an artisan coffee and viennoiserie, were rapidly evaporating.

"Drebar mana?" Romy recalled a burly Malay bloke who would likely have been more adept in dealing with emergency services than this, albeit amiable, imp.

"PKPD di Selangor, Boss, dia tak boleh mari kerja."

Romy debated between offering the fella a ride, either to the hospital or to the police station, when the latter decided for him, which was neither.

"I sikit kena kaki saje, Boss. Lebih bayek kita balik ke rumah. Boleh tolong kita, plis Boss."

Romy stood silently for a moment. He was in two minds.

On the left was the lorong leading to the bakery. A line of cars was inching their way forward, looking for parking spots. The chalkboard by the entrance was already in place, with the selection of breads available scrawled all over it. He could actually smell the aroma of coffee. If he were to make a guess, it was likely medium roast, Colombian beans.

On the right was the lane which led to the tai tai's mansion at the top of the hill. Hardly anyone traversed along it, as the properties were large and far between.

Romy hesitated. He was torn between which road to take. He frowned, which the wily little shrimp took for a yes.

Actually, there was one other thing bugging Romy: He couldn't remember the joker's name.

For some reason, that song with the distorted guitar accompaniment kept playing in his head. *If I could, then I would... I'll go wherever you will go...* Heck, what was the name of the band that sang it? Urrgh, his memory. *Zul Ariffin bod with a Joe Biden brain, damnit.* He gave up.

"I tak ingat lagi nama you."

Another toothy smile from his newly reconnected friend. "Bilal."

Of course. That was it. The Calling.

$$\times$$

Romy's previous impression of the humongous house had not wavered. It was as hideous as he had remembered.

But it had not always been so.

Originally a graceful example of Art Deco streamlined geometry, it had been a gentle ode to the elegant halcyon days of British presence in pre-independent Malaya. The perfect connector between classical and modern.

Then along came a superstitious Cina singkek, who made his money by – hell, nobody had ever quite fathomed how he made his money, but he had a lot of it. And each time AMLA came into the picture, the key witnesses mysteriously ended up incapacitated or dead and the enforcement team had no choice but to stamp the file NFA.

Ah Sing's purchase of the property was simply because it was south-facing and the lot no. had an '8' in it.

Akin to gifting a masterpiece to Mr. Bean, Ah Sing had proceeded to renovate the house in his own image. Which, to put it facetiously as an analogy, no offense, but his poor mother had probably only experienced morning sickness after he was born, rather than before.

He'd spared many of the trees in the garden, though. Some of them were increasingly rare. Romy recognized several species, including the pokok keruing, damar minyak, kepayang and the ever-sought-after gaharu.

As careful with his health as he was with his money, Ah Sing had enjoyed a long life. Perhaps the verb 'enjoy' was subjective. It was difficult to imagine how any man could have found marital bliss with the tai tai. Shy to say aloud in these politically correct times and not to knock women, but to paraphrase the Bard, two words which came to mind when describing the tai tai were jew and shrew.

It humbled one into thinking that, in a mysterious way, God was indeed fair.

One of the security guards immediately pressed the remote switch to open the gold on gold, trackless folding gates as they arrived. But Romy insisted on parking outside the property. He didn't want to presume he would be bestowed the same savior's welcome with which Bilal had fêted him.

In this instance, he wasn't too worried about his Ativa. Heck, this was Kenny Hills what.

A tall, lean young man in an Armani polo shirt featuring an eagle logo and emoji patches was on the steps leading to the portico, just before the double front doors. His loose fit denim jeans were seriously worn, not as a matter of style but because they were authentically vintage. He had probably worn them a few hundred times over the years.

There was a shorter, plump man beside him, wearing a basic Nike x Stüssy tee with 'INCREASE THE PEACE' blazoned across it and a pair of Le Coq Sportif joggers. It didn't look like he'd done any jogging that morning, though. Nor on any other morning, for that matter.

They were obviously brothers, likely in their twenties. Their masks were at chin level but they hastily hitched them up when they saw Romy. He had a vague recollection, on his previous visit, of there having been a mention of grandchildren away at boarding school in a neighboring state.

"Ah Inspector, you're here on your own?" the tall one asked first. "I always thought you guys worked in pairs. Been watching too many crime dramas," he chuckled.

"No, actually, I –" Romy attempted to explain but the short one interjected, "Quick, Inspector! Upstairs! We need to break down the bedroom door."

There was nothing for Romy to do but follow them as they raced up to the room in question, with Bilal and the two security guards tailing behind.

The rest of the household staff were too stricken to do anything other than huddle together at the top of the sweeping U-shaped staircase, a tacky imitation of the one at Tara, in *Gone with the Wind*, as they watched the drama enfold.

A non-binary in a slouchy black Bozz t-shirt and Kirrin Finch coral pink chino shorts was sobbing hysterically outside the door. Their multi-colored pixie cut and tanzanite nose stud set off a trippy vibe. "It's locked and bolted from inside, Sergeant. I've banged and banged but Po Po's not answering."

"I'm not from the pol–" Romy tried again, as the tall guy said, "Inspector, it's okay. Yes, we're aware that, as this is our grandmother's house, in the event of insurance claims, we're required to have a special permit to break down the door –"

As before, the short dude interrupted with, "Inspector, sibs, we don't have time to chat, maa!" And proceeded to smash the door with a hammer.

The door was of solid teak from the rainforests of Sulawesi. It put up a plucky fight but proved to be a poor match against the onslaught of Shorty's hammerific blows.

The bruised and battered door hit the citrine colored granite floor with a crash.

After the frenzied efforts to gain entry to the room, everyone was suddenly hesitant and drew back.

Eventually, the still-bawling gender-fluid person picked their way tentatively over the fallen door and ran in.

"Hazelyn, wait!" the elder of their brothers advised.

Their loud gasp of horror was suffice preparation for the worst.

The tai tai was lying on the Tianjin silk rug by the bed at the far end of the room. It was obvious she had suffered some sort of seizure, as her facial features were contorted in agony. An unpleasant odor permeating from her long, loose (dare one say, pasar malam) kaftan, which had partly ridden up her knees, indicated she had soiled herself in the process.

There was an overturned Lalique tumbler of water beside her. It must have fallen from the bedside table.

Romy pressed his fingers on the old crone's wrist and then at the side of her neck. At the same time, he noted a faint aroma of what, in wine connoisseur parlance, would be termed a marzipan nose.

There was no pulse.

He shook his head. "I would say death likely occurred some hours ago. See the arms and legs? Rigor mortis has already set in."

Hazelyn immediately burst into a fresh torrent of weeping, beating their chest with their hands.

"Po Po! Noooo!" they wailed without inhibition.

Their brothers tried to console them. "Hazelyn, it's okay, it's okay."

But they pushed their brothers violently away, blubbering unashamedly like a child.

Romy felt faintly embarrassed. He wasn't meant to be here, anyway. Besides, it was his birthday, fuckitt. He tried to tiptoe away discreetly.

The tall dude called him back. "Inspector, where are you going?"

Damn, this was just like a Mr. Bean moment of mistaken identity.

$$\times$$

It was half an hour later.

In the smallest of the four ostentatiously furnished reception areas of the house, PI Romy found himself seated on an intricately hand-carved Qianlong period sofa with carvings of stylized dragons and other mythical beasts centered on its back.

Across from him, on walnut wood chairs also carved with dragons, but etched with shou (longevity) medallions along the arms, sat both brothers.

The tall one, he discovered, was Ashyon and his short brother was Dickson.

Their siblings, Hazelyn and Judith, lounged on embroidered silk and brocade floor cushions slightly further away, gesturing and whispering to each other woefully in Chinese.

They had dispensed with face masks. After all, they were at home and had already received their double dose, maa. Romy kept his mask on, he still had another appointment to go for his second jab.

Now it was Judith's turn to be upset at the tragedy that had befallen. Romy cast a discreet glance at her for the first time.

The antithesis of her gender-fluid sibling, Judith was equally striking to look at, garbed in an Ellie Dress by Mister Zimi and an Erdem embellished ribbon headband that resembled a halo. She looked like a cross between a Victoria's Secret angel and a Talking Barbie doll. Her double eyelids drooped down to display her impossibly lush eyelashes, as a crocodile formation of perfectly forged tears rolled down her Anastasia Beverly Hills Blush Trio-sculpted cheeks.

Romy had never seen anyone cry so elegantly. He wished he had a handkerchief on him to offer to dry her tears.

Hazelyn, on the other hand, appeared to have recovered their composure and placed a comforting roped forearm with a tattoo of a snake and a lotus glowing on their wrist, round their distraught younger sister.

"I'm going to miss Po Po so much," Judith wept, scrunching her seraphic features endearingly in a spasm of sniveling.

When Romy had finally managed to blurt out that he wasn't a police inspector, to his surprise, they had been curiously unduly relieved. In fact there was a noticeable lightening in the atmosphere.

"We just want to know who killed our grandmother for our own peace of mind, PI Romy," Ashyon declared. "No need to involve the police. Po Po was old, anyway."

"It's an offense to conceal a suspicious death," Romy pointed out, in a burst of civic duty and moral conscience.

Hazelyn declared stiffly, "Po Po is a private citizen what, and her death is a family matter. She's not a public figure that her cause of death must be made known to the whole world."

"Was," Dickson corrected them automatically. "Po Po is in the past tense now. Anyway, old people sometimes, they just die."

Romy couldn't help noticing the element of glee in his voice.

"There's something not quite right in the manner she died," Ashyon insisted. "PI Romy, you do agree with me?"

"Uh," Romy hesitated. "Well, um, as Mr. Dickson said, old people sometimes just die." He knew he was now definitely failing in his public duty. But frankly, he didn't much care to be involved. Futtocks, it was his birthday.

Yet out of habit, when he'd encountered the victim, Romy had made a quick mental note of all the details relating to the crime scene.

It was a large room but made to feel cramped, because it was simply groaning with furniture. There were outsized camphor wood chests edged in brass, a colossal cedar wood and jade lacquered screen, a goodly number of mother of pearl inlay tables, a pair of massive antique rosewood dressers and ewwh… were those a row of vintage porcelain chamber pots?

There were also several Ji Chi Mu (Phoenix tail wood) wardrobes, which housed an impressive collection of evening dresses and accessories. One of the wardrobes was so chock-full of stuff, its door didn't shut properly. A whiff of mothballs floated out from within its cavernous interior.

The guards had made an immediate inspection to ensure nobody was hiding behind the screen or in one of the chests. But everything appeared to be neatly arranged and in order.

Dickson had removed the distraught Hazelyn from the room, while Ashyon had instructed the nurse Porntip to clean up their grandmother a little and to dress her in a more presentable outfit.

His voice was loud and and authoritative. "I think the Yeohlee Teng black and ivory evening dress will do nicely for Madame, Porntip. Lay Madame on the Peranakan four poster bed in the Magenta bedroom. The red and gold bed," he reminded her, indicating that there was more than one bed in there.

He motioned to the trio of Filipina maids hovering about. "Perdita, Felizia, Carmen, help Porntip. Ezekiel, Yeshua," – these were the security guards – "search the grounds, in case anyone is still lurking there. Unlikely, though. Bilal, you go knock on Miss Judith's door, wake her up. How she can sleep through this racket, I don't know. Then tell Ah Foong to make us some coffee."

Yes, coffee. Romy decided he could do with one, the image of his elusive Cortado morphing into a kopi gah dai. The sugar rush in it was exactly what he needed.

But when the steaming cup of aromatic locally brewed kopi was finally placed on the fine, low satinwood table beside him, he couldn't drink it. A pantang about not partaking of food or beverage when there was a death in the house.

"We have a coffee factory in Mantin. It's our own blend, try it," urged Dickson.

Aah, so that was one of the ways the crafty Ah Sing had legitimized his ill-gotten gains.

"We use only premium New Zealand butter when roasting and our beans are ground with a mill grinder, so the coffee is a consistent size. We sell close to 50 million packs of ground coffee in a year, all over the world."

"Jesus-Joseph-Mary and the wee donkey," interpolated Ashyon. "Po Po just died and still you have to talk shop."

"No need to swear, it's not that deep," Judith snapped unexpectedly from her corner. Her halo was slipping.

"Sis is right," bleated Dickson. "Life goes on. And like I tell you, old people sometimes just die. What to do!" He sounded almost ecstatic.

Ashyon lifted his hands in a pleading gesture. "PI Romy, our grandmother was a very private person, so we would like to honor her passing in a dignified way. We definitely don't want an autopsy. That would be xia suay. But we need to know if there was any foul play involved. For our own peace of mind."

Now it was Hazelyn's turn to snap. "Ah Yon, why you have to be so kepoh, haa?"

"Well, in these chaotic times, I don't know, people may do something idiotic, which they regret. But it's too late," Ashyon remarked gravely.

"If too late, then what's the point of investigating?" clucked Dickson impatiently. "Fuckaduck, it's like going on a wild goose chase."

"Ya lor, I don't understand Ashyon's logic," agreed Hazelyn. "Thinks he's so smart."

"Sibs, ple-ee-ease! Let's not bicker. In the end, all we have is each other." Judith's halo was firmly back in position.

Family politics, thought Romy to himself. At the same time, his curiosity was kindled. "How about your parents?" he asked Ashyon. "They're not here?"

"Divorced when we were young. Mama lives in Dublin, we think. She hasn't been in touch. Papa quarreled with Ah Kong and emigrated to Perth. He died last year."

Poor little rich kids. Still, he had to ask. "You all never thought of moving to Australia, too? Could have got your PR quite easily."

They stared at him as if he'd gone mad.

"Why in heaven's name would we do that?" asked Ashyon.

"So hard just to find a teh tarik in Murdoch or Northbridge even, let alone a decent nasi lemak in the whole of Perth," quipped Dickson.

Romy made up his mind. "I charge by the hour. And I'll need a room where I can interview each person."

Suddenly, all the siblings were wary. Hazelyn and Judith exchanged cryptic glances. Dickson opened his mouth to say something, then evidently thought better of it. Even Ashyon didn't seem so confident that it was the right thing.

It was several seconds before Ashyon replied. "Yes, sure. Er… how many hours do you estimate it will take for you to find out, PI Romy?"

Oh man, the guy's faith in my detective skills is touching, thought Romy. Aloud he said nonchalantly and immediately regretted it, "Oh, not long. Before lunchtime."

Damn, he was really getting ahead of himself.

$$\times$$

Ashyon allocated Romy the den in the basement to conduct his investigations.

It was a windowless room with charcoal gray walls, theater style seating and a massive Samsung MicroLED home cinema display. Its stark atmosphere suited Romy's purpose perfectly.

He requested for an upright chair to be brought in and placed facing the seats, to conduct his interviews.

He decided to start with the Filipina trio first. They flounced in, like pumped-up hopefuls in a *Philippines Got Talent* TV show.

They were cooperative but unhelpful. Everything was same-same as always. They had gone about their household duties and tried to keep out of Ma'am's way.

"Ma'am very strict, izzit?" Romy knew the answer. He had asked the question in the previous investigation but decided to throw in the question again anyway.

Felizia, the most vocal of the three, played with a lock of her L'Oreal Babylon Intense Red-dyed hair and declared, "She's even more crazy krung krung now. Even when we do our work properly, she is shouting and scolding."

"She's already dead, Feli," giggled Perdita. "You must say, Ma'am *was* more crazy."

Carmen, the timid and youngest one of the trio, looked as though she was about to speak, then changed her mind.

Romy let them go.

Next he interviewed the cook, Ah Foong.

She had been on leave for the Cheng Beng festival at the time of the missing pearls, so this was his first meeting with her.

To his surprise, he noted her eyes were swollen from crying. "Your boss was good to you?"

Ah Foong nodded and her face crumpled. "Thirty years I here. I come when I fifteen. My hometown Sitiawan. Same as Mama hometown. But we like to say it as City A One," she added proudly.

"Oh, you called your boss, Mama?"

"Ya, she like a mother to me, lor. To the chirren oso, she try so hard but they always complain she too strict. Compare her with their Ah Kong. He spoil them so much, they were so sad when he die. I hear one of them say, why couldn't it be Mama who die. So bad, they all. But Mama, you know, dia macam orang Melayu kata, dalam hati ada taman."

Romy played devil's advocate. "But the other maids say, Mama was er… siao."

Ah Foong curled her lip. "Huh, they all very lansi, always want to ekshen. Make Mama kan cheong." She leaned forward in a confiding manner. "You know, I tell you. These Philippines women got no shame, one. Bring Bangladeshi boyfriend come into the house at night to kongkek."

"When? Last night?"

Ah Foong sat back dramatically in her chair. "Every night, maa!"

The security guards, Yeshua and Ezekiel were next on Romy's list. They greeted Romy like an old friend and answered his questions readily.

No, they had not seen anyone suspicious hanging about outside the property. Besides, there were also regular patrols in the vicinity by various security companies.

And Yeshua often enjoyed helping to prune the ivy which grew all along the walls of the compound. He would definitely have spotted anything out of the ordinary.

They took it in turns to be on the night shift. Although it wasn't his turn, Ezekiel had done the patrols round the compound hourly, the previous night.

"Because I have stomach ache," explained Yeshua.

Romy couldn't help noticing a large hickey on Yeshua's earlobe but made no comment. It was already a few days old, anyway.

As expected, they expressed astonishment and disbelief at the accusation leveled at the Pinoys by Ah Foong.

Romy knew, too, it was unlikely either of the guards had anything to do with the murder. It would have been too extreme. They had extended families in the interior of Sabah who depended on the wages they sent back.

He decided to sound out Bilal. The artful dodger merely looked vague and repeated unconvincingly that he knew nothing of such goings-ons. He was a pious man and "You tau Boss, ghibah dan fitnah itu dosa besar, Boss."

Ghibah wasn't a word Romy was familiar with. He guessed it meant the same as mengumpat. To keep the matter at hand on a professional keel, he reverted to English. "How was Mem's behaviour the last few days?"

"Normal, Boss. Cerewet macam biasa. Kasi kita suma pening. But this her house, Boss. Dia senang boleh buat apa dia suka."

"Don't the grandchildren have any share in the property? What about the money their grandfather left behind?"

Bilal miraculously set aside his views on ghibah. "Itu sumua Mem control. Of course, if Mem die, lain cerita. Everything meant to go to them. But I hear lah, Boss, baru-baru ni, Mem very angry with one of the grandchildren, want to change her will. Make appointment to see lawyer but because of PKP, lawyer office close. Driver oso cannot coming to drive Mem. So belum boleh jumpa lawyer lagi."

"Oh."

Romy was silent for a bit. Then he tried another tack.

"Miss Judith. Is she a very heavy sleeper… yang jenis tidur mati ke? Always wake up late?"

"No, Boss. Biasanya, pagi-pagi Miss Judith sudah jalan-jalan in garden. Tapi, last night dia kata dia ambil itu sleeping pill. That's why just now I knocking her door many time, then only I hear her 'on' the tap very loud in bathroom."

Romy nodded to indicate that was all for the time being.

He decided he would take another peek at the crime scene before questioning the nurse. Not that he was hopeful of discovering anything new.

He took in the details of the room, as he had remembered them earlier. The room had been left as it was. Only the broken door had been moved neatly to one side for easy access.

It was a shame, though, that the items of furniture, each an exquisite example of bespoke craftsmanship, should be crammed together in a jumble to resemble the interior of a junk store.

The old lady had never been known to lock her bedroom door, much less bolt it. Quite regularly, she needed to use the bathroom in the night and the nurse would be summoned by the buzzer to help her.

The window shades had been left open as they always were. Ashyon had explained it was because their grandmother preferred to awaken naturally by the early morning light streaming in through the windows. It was also a sheer forty foot drop from the windows, down to the stone courtyard below.

So this was the classic impossible crime mystery. There was no way the perpetrator could have entered the room, committed the murder and then left again, with the door locked and bolted from the inside.

Romy stood for several moments, lost in thought.

A voice at his side made him start. It was the nurse.

"PI Lomy, I waiting for you downstair so long, you never come." Her limpid caramel brown eyes looked at him reproachfully.

Nice contacts, Romy observed irrelevantly. "Uhh? Okay, Miss Porntip, I ask you some questions now."

He ushered her to a pair of Zitan wood and marble-inlaid throne style armchairs with chrysanthemum and bird motifs, in the middle of the room. The upholstered seat made it bearable for his butt but it was helluva uncomfortable for his back.

Damnit, was it his imagination or was she leaning a little too close to him? "You are feeling fine, PI Lomy?" she asked anxiously.

Heck, she was a nurse, after all. "Ya."

He got down to business.

"So, what time did you last see Madame?" He remembered in time that the Thais, like their Indo-Chinese neighbors, preferred to say 'Madame'.

"After Madame finish watch TV. She sit here to watch where we sit now, actually," Porntip giggled shyly, whereas others might have found it macabre.

"What time was that?"

Porntip paused a while as she tried to recall. "After movie finish at aloun' midnigh' maybe."

"Which movie?"

"The new one on Mubi. It call… oh solly, I no lemember. Madame call me help her go toilet after movie. Then I think she leading Bible until she fall asleep. Sometime she wake up in nigh', wan' go toilet again. But not las' nigh'. I wait her to call me in morning when she wake up but still she don't call."

The realization why Madame hadn't called, suddenly hit her and she began to cry.

"Madame was a kind employer?" Romy dropped the question casually.

Porntip dried her eyes with a tissue. "Madame she is – was – not a happy person. A person who is unhappy will fine it not easy to be kine, PI Lomy."

"Maybe." It wasn't within his job spec to go into anything holistic or spiritual like that. He asked her another question. "Does Madame drink alcohol? Like red wine, for example. It's meant to be good for the heart."

Porntip nodded. "Yes. Sometime, one of the chirlen come to Madame loom, they talk an' dlink together." She hesitated. "But las' nigh', no. No, Madame was alone."

"I see. How about you? Where do you sleep?"

"My loom nex' to Madame."

A thought struck him. "Mx. Hazelyn and Miss Judith's bedrooms. Are they near to Madame's?"

"Miss Judith, her loom also nex' to Madame room, the other si'e. Mx. Hazely' loom is opposite Madame loom, besi'e Magenta loom."

"And Mr. Ashyon and Mr. Dickson?"

"Madame angly they like to play dlum velly lou'. So they stay in annexe acloss flom swimming pool."

"I see." Romy glanced quickly round the room as they got up to leave it. The offending wardrobe door was still a wafer-thin width ajar.

He decided to prise it open to see what it contained, before banging it shut completely. The culprit was a large tapestry bedspread which had been carelessly stuffed in the wardrobe, so that its tasseled fringe had caught in the bottom edge of the door.

Romy dragged the whole bedspread out to see if there was anything else in the wardrobe. There was nothing, save for a miniature empty liqueur bottle. From the Lombardy region in north Italy.

Romy had actually spent a couple of months there, early in his military career. One of those G to G exchanges, where his infantry was sent to train in the Italian Alps, and their Italian counterparts were plonked in the mountainous region of Sabah.

Freezing his arse off, the odd swig of Amaretto, for which Lombardy was famous, had helped.

He tucked the empty bottle in his pocket. Aloud he said, "Just a final question, Miss Porntip. Why is that bedroom called Magenta?"

She paused before replying. "I hear it was Madame daughter-in-law room. Her name Magenta. Madame hate her so much, she say because Magenta steal her tings. But Mx. Hazely' say Madame no like their mother because she is a farang – how you say in Malay – mat salleh. So I no understan' why, now that Madame die, Mr. Ashyon wan' to place Madame on his mother's bed and make Madame wear his mother's clothing."

✕

Romy could hear conversational noises coming from the dining room.

As he made his way in its direction, Carmen the timid one beckoned to him from the entrance hall, where she was wiping the collection of Song dynasty Cizhou ware on the hongmu meditation table.

"I have something I must tell you, Sir," she whispered urgently.

Motioning to him to follow, she led him to a small recessed alcove, framed incongruously by a pair of Doric columns, where they could be safely out of sight and hearing. "Okay, what izzit?"

"I was mopping the corridor upstairs outside the bedrooms yesterday, Sir."

"Ya, so?"

"Porntip was in Mx. Hazelyn's room. Sir, they sounded like they were arguing. Then I heard Porntip saying many times to Mx. Hazelyn, 'you lie, you lie!' Ma'am was coming upstairs and she heard it too. Sir, I think Ma'am was angry. So I quickly went downstairs again, out of her way. Later, Porntip told me Ma'am was sending her back to Thailand. Porntip was very sad because she has a sick Mom and needs the money to buy her Mom's medicine."

Romy nodded thoughtfully. "Thank you, Miss Carmen. You've been very helpful indeed."

He smiled and continued on his way to the dining room. As he glanced at the early 19th century Qianlong ormolu musical clock on the Qing period green and gold lacquered apothecary cabinet, it chimed the half hour. It was coming close to lunchtime.

Romy felt suddenly irritated. He still had one more piece to find to complete the puzzle. But how?

Damnit, chasing waterfalls, not murderers, was how he'd planned to spend his birthday morning. Except, perhaps in this instance, there was something apt in that song by TLC, expressing how people chased impalpable dreams with no thought of the consequences.

To err on the side of civic duty, he rapidly keyed in a quick message to his Inspector friend at the Tun Razak balai. The latter would know to contact his Sentul counterpart to do the necessary.

In the dining room, the siblings were seated round the Ming design elm wood oval dining table, the remains of a late breakfast in their bowls.

A death in the family had given them a voracious appetite.

Except for Hazelyn, who had no bowl, just a half-drunk glass of carrot juice. They tapped its rim with their forefinger in a fidgety gesture.

Judith saw him first and pointed guiltily at the large phoenix and peony porcelain tureen on the lazy Susan. "Oh, I'm so sorry, PI Romy. We were having bak kut teh."

He smiled candidly at her. "There's no need to apologize to me for that, Miss Judith."

Inwardly, he marveled how those of other faiths were so respectful of his religion. The average Malay person would think nothing of tucking into a good beef rendang in the company of Hindus and Buddhists. That it might be deemed insensitive or even offensive seldom occurred to the Malay psyche.

It was food for thought.

"And for Bilal, he has his own small kitchen to cook his meals," she added hastily.

You don't have to tell me and I don't need to know, thought Romy. *So he and I are brothers in Islam, but I'm not his keeper. Neither is he mine.* Instead he remarked politely, "Your bak kut teh looks very different from the norm. My mother makes chi kut teh sometimes, that's how I know."

"Yes, it's a traditional family recipe from our Ah Kong's side," Judith replied conversationally. "We put buah keluak in it. From the kepayang trees in our garden. They've been bearing fruit nonstop lately because of the dry weather. I supervise Yeshua myself to pluck the fruit with a galah."

Romy was glancing idly at an open laptop on the marble-topped Chinoiserie sideboard, with its screensaver still on. He turned his full attention to confirm what she had just said, "Yeshua, the security guard?"

"Yes," Judith went on in her mostest hostess manner. "His kampung in Sipitang has plenty of kepayang trees too."

But Romy had lost interest. Instead he asked, "Whose laptop is that one?"

"Po Po's," Hazelyn piped up drily. "It was for her online Bible study meetings. But if you ask me, some of them in the group spend more time dissing other people's grandchildren than discussing the Word of God."

"Hazelyn, what an unkind thing to say!" admonished Judith, shocked.

"It happens among other religious study circles too," Romy agreed with Hazelyn.

Memories of his ex-mother-in-law discussing his marital problems in such detail with her usrah circle, so that his ex-wife-to-be had even suggested calling off their divorce proceedings to shut up the makcik-makcik, came back to him.

"Well, PI Romy?" Ashyon wiped his hands on a Caspari Summer Palace paper napkin and then blew his nose into it. "Any leads?"

Romy looked at him contemplatively for a couple of seconds. "Even better, Sir," he replied airily. "I've solved the matter."

"It's not murder, then?" Dickson cried out eagerly.

Oh my, what a high voice you have, Mr. D, said Romy softly to himself. He addressed Dickson directly. "I'm afraid it is."

"Impossible," Dickson exclaimed incredulously. "A door locked and bolted from the inside. Windows impossible to enter or to go out of. No way ho zayy. It has to be how I said at the beginning, PI Romy. Old people sometimes just die."

At the word "die", Hazelyn burst into a fresh flood of tears, gesticulating wildly, "Don't say that word!"

"Look what you've done! You're a real cili api!" their sister chided, wagging an admonishing finger at Dickson. "You've upset them again."

Of course. That was it! The Pointer Sisters! *Fire.*

So I got that sorted too, thought Romy smugly. No need to text AP after all.

"Let's all gather together in the den, PI Romy," Ashyon suggested. "With the servants, as well. I suppose one of them is the murderer. It will be harder for whoever it is to make a quick getaway when we're in there."

"Oh no, that won't be necessary, Sir," said Romy. "The murderer is actually among us now. It's one of you."

$$\times$$

What an unusual birthday morning it had been, mused Romy, as he collected his Grab food delivery from his front door and proceeded to sit down and enjoy it. *But then it's a strange world we live in now*, he sighed inwardly.

He had decided to treat himself to a proper Italian meal.

From Porto Romano, no less.

Stuffed mussels to start with, then cream of broccoli soup, followed by squid ink pasta with calamari rings, and a bowl of panna cotta as a sweet ending.

Feeling blissfully content after his midday banquet, he relived the moments when he dramatically revealed the tragic circumstances that had led to the tai tai's agonizing and untimely death.

*Indubitably one of my prouder moments in my career as a Private Investigato*r, he decided. How eloquent he had sounded!

Marrying an English-language teacher had not been wasted.

It had been similar to something straight out of a film. Like that send up of the classic country house murder mystery with Daniel Craig. It had been an unexpected blockbuster at the cinema a few years ago.

The cinema.

Damn.

At the rate the Covid was messing with 'life' as everyone had known it, the next gen were going to wonder what a cinema was. Same way some kids these days had never seen a real telephone.

"Ladies and gentlemen," he had announced, rubbing his hands together. "I admit I was initially –" he sought for a fancy word, mindful that this was Kenny Hills. "I was initially flummoxed by the curious circumstances of this case. By golly, it appeared to be the perfect impossible crime."

He warmed up to his theme.

"To be frank, I was unsure if I could solve it. But with my expertise and time-tested skills as a private investigator to the A-list and the A-leet, I am happy to report that I uh… cracked it." Romy was running out of steam, but momentarily.

"Like every good detective worth his, her, or their salt, I embarked on my quest, looking for even the smallest of clues. And because of my relentless pursuit in leaving no stone unturned, I was amply rewarded."

By then, Romy's little audience of four was beginning to get restless.

"If you don't mind, can you just get to the point please, PI Romy?" Hazelyn had suggested in a dangerously polite tone.

"Bear with me while, Mx.," Romy had bowed gravely in turn. "I am getting there. My first clue was when I was checking your recently departed grandmother for a pulse. Despite the odor emanating from her… er… nether orifices, I was able to detect an aroma of almonds coming from the deceased's mouth area."

He had then paused for effect, at the same time making a mental observation of their individual reactions.

Ashyon had appeared to be the only one paying attention. Dickson had looked blur, Hazelyn had appeared bored and Judith's seraphic expression indicated that her thoughts were obviously elsewhere.

Nevertheless, Romy had continued stoically. "The next stage of my quest was to interrogate the household staff. I am happy to record that they were of enormous assistance to my progress on the case. Enormous assistance," Romy had repeated, and paused again for effect.

But everyone had looked as though they honestly couldn't have cared less.

"How so, PI Romy?" The grudging tone in Ashyon's voice made it obvious that he had felt obliged to ask.

Romy had merely smiled in a self-deprecating manner but did not elaborate. "For my next clue, I re-examined the crime scene. And I appreciate very much that you had left it as it was. It clarified a key point in my investigations."

A discernible shift in the mood of those present was evident.

Dickson, for one, couldn't contain his curiosity. "What did you find, PI Romy?"

But Romy had merely made a steeple of his fingers and smiled yet again.

Absentmindedly chewing the side of his thumbnail, Ashyon had kept his gaze on the Lim Ah Cheng semi-abstract oil painting of galloping horses on the wall.

Hazelyn's look on their face was such that they would've slapped Romy, given the chance.

Judith emerged from her dream world, opened her eyes very wide and appeared surprised to find herself seated where she was.

Meanwhile, Dickson had burst out, "Why won't you just tell us, man?"

"In good time, Mr. Dickson, in good time," Romy's demeanor was so calm and reassuring, he was beginning to sound like an obstetrician.

"So!" He had continued his narrative. "I was on my way from your Po Po's room to meet with all of you here in the dining room to discuss my findings, when one of the staff approached me with additional information. Information which was indeed vital. But there was still a missing link toward solving the mystery until –"

In the manner of a clairvoyant divining tea leaves at the bottom of a cup, Romy had pointed theatrically at the large tureen of now nearly-empty bak kut teh in the center of the table, "I saw *that*."

Everyone had automatically craned their necks to look into the contents of the tureen, and then simultaneously turned to stare blankly at him.

Romy took out the tiny empty bottle of liqueur from his pocket and deliberately placed it beside the tureen.

The puzzled expressions of his audience of four changed to utter bewilderment. One of them was faking it pretty well.

"To explain it in a nutshell, your Po Po was murdered using cyanide extracted from the buah keluak in her garden."

"What?!" Ashyon's incredulous expression had appeared genuine.

"But Po Po never liked buah keluak," countered Hazelyn. "She said it tasted like mud."

"We like it though, and we eat it so often. If it's poisonous as you say, we should all be dead now," Dickson had chuckled humorlessly.

"I'm talking about buah keluak in its natural form," Romy had explained. "It's like a cyanide ball unless it's properly fermented. To make buah keluak edible, you need to boil the fruit, coat it in ash, then bury it in the ground for a few weeks."

"Okay, so you're saying one of us gave some fresh buah keluak to Po Po to eat. Just laidat." Ashyon's Malaysian voice of reason prompted Romy to descend a few rungs from the lofty heights of his 'world's greatest detective' mode.

"Er... ya, sumting laidat," agreed Romy, dropping his pretentious illusions of atas-ness, to even his own relief.

"How?" challenged Dickson.

"Actually, it was put in her liqueur."

"Her Amaretto? Yes, Po Po always enjoyed a night time tipple," Judith reminisced sadly.

Romy pointed at the contents of the label on the bottle. "This particular brand is made from almonds. Buah keluak has a bitter nutty taste, which should blend in quite well. Your Po Po wouldn't have noticed anything amiss when she drank it."

"So it was quite painless then, her death," remarked Dickson, flippantly. As if he cared.

"Oh no," Romy had corrected him. "She would have begun feeling dizzy and breathless. She may have tried to summon help, that's how the tumbler of water got knocked over. But it wouldn't have made a difference. Shortly after, she would have had convulsions and started vomiting. Eventually, because her body cells couldn't get oxygen, she would have passed out and then died. It would have been a horrible and painful death."

"Oh that's too, too awful!" Judith's eyes were filled with tears. "Who could have been so cruel to inflict that on Po Po?"

Romy's voice had been emotionless. "Someone who despised your grandmother for her old-fashioned ideals. Who saw her as an obstacle to any chance of happiness in living life according to one's choice of partner. Your Po Po, I understand, was having serious thoughts about changing her will. But a new, even more stringent lockdown was suddenly imposed yet again, which meant the lawyer's office was closed. So there was a small window of opportunity for the killer to strike, before law firms inevitably open again. But it had to be done swiftly. That's the beauty of cyanide poisoning. It's not easy to determine. The victim would appear to have maybe just suffered a fatal stroke or a heart attack, especially if she's elderly. All of you are aware of your grandmother often having a nightcap at bedtime, and you would take it in turns to join her. But it seems, not last night. According to Porntip, your grandmother spent the whole evening on her own."

Romy had paused for effect. The suspense. Man, he was getting good at this.

"But Porntip lied to me. One of you did go into your Po Po's room. Maybe to say sorry for what happened earlier in the day and make amends over a bottle of Amaretto, Po Po's favorite. Likely it reminded her of Italy, where she'd studied Opera many years ago at the Conservatorio in Milan. But this one had been infused with buah keluak. So it was ciao bella to poor Po Po."

"How do you explain the locked and bolted door from the inside? When we all entered the room, there was nobody in there except Po Po," challenged Hazelyn. "I saw for myself, maa."

Romy had emitted a long low chuckle. "Ah yes. The impossible crime. A murder is committed and the murderer vanishes into thin air. Songlap! But not so impossible if we consider the circumstances. Everyone is in a panic. Kelam kabut. All attention is on Po Po. True, a search was done of the room but it's so easy to miss details. I mean, you all go in and out of your grandmother's room so often, you take it for granted. It's stuffed with furniture and her cupboards are filled with all her things. So a quick glance round is enough to satisfy that all is in order. Remember, you're all of you in shock. Easy to overlook if there's anything out of place. And so, nobody thinks of looking behind the bedspread that's stuffed in the wardrobe. Just nice for our murderer to hide. Then when the hoo ha is over and everyone has left the room, it's kacang for him or her or they, to tiptoe out again."

"Okay, if it happened as you said, which one of us did it?" asked Ashyon. "We were all there."

"And if you're going to say Judith wasn't, we know she was in her room," Dickson was quick to come to his sister's defense. "When Bilal knocked on her door, he could hear the shower running."

"Why do I get the feeling that you think I killed my grandmother, PI Romy?" Hazelyn's tone was insolent as well as bored. "Because I found her to be an obstacle to my happiness? Okay lah, so my gender identity and expression was at odds with her traditional thinking and orthodox religious beliefs. But it's not a strong enough motive for me to kill her."

"Ya, it has to be more than that," agreed Romy. "As it happens, Mx. Hazelyn, Carmen had told me she overheard Porntip accusing you of lying. In actual fact, Porntip was saying, 'You like?' It's the Thai accent when speaking English, you see. The consonants at the ends of words tend to be omitted. So let's just keep it to, uh, how do I put it, you and Porntip were having a good time in your room, while Carmen was cleaning the corridor. Unfortunately your grandmother came upstairs looking for Porntip, as her online Bible study meeting must have ended earlier than usual. She was so repulsed when she discovered your liaison, she swore she was going to cut you out of her will."

Hazelyn couldn't contain themself anymore. "Yeah, that holier-than-thou, kerepot old sow! How dare she want to deny me my rightful inheritance! Asking me again and again, 'Why are you gae? Why are you gae?' It's the same as wanting to know how come her eyes are so slitty one. Urrgh. Preaching to me about divine wrath and eternal damnation. Insisting I go see a psychiatrist!" Hazelyn paused for breath and continued with a defiant swagger, "Okay, so I did go into her room last night."

"Hazelyn!" Ashyon was aghast.

His sibling turned to him fiercely. "And yeah, I pretended I was sorry and promised to repent. But that's as far as it went. I swear on Ah Kong's soul. Po Po was very much alive and watching a movie on TV when I left her."

"If not you, then, who?" squeaked Dickson, sounding as though he were accusing someone of stealing a cookie from the cookie pot. "You had the motive, Hae."

Hazelyn raked their fingers through their lavender, pink and blue streaked hair in despair. "Look, aiyah, I can't explain it. I know it does seem like it would be me. But I did not kill Po Po. I mean, she took care of us all when Ma abandoned us and Pa decided he was done with Ah Kong and everything here. I loved Po Po, despite her bigoted ass mind. Uhh, what can I say, it's complicated."

"Doesn't matter what you say, Haze," put in Judith mildly. "But it does matter what you did. The Amaretto bottle you left in the wardrobe is proof of that."

Romy smiled in a self-satisfied manner. He had finally reached the end of his pursuit. If he were Brad, he would've licked his face with his paws and purred. His tone was silky. "But Miss Judith, how did you know the bottle was in the wardrobe? I never said that it was."

Judith's delicately coated Shiseido pixel pink gel lipsticked lower lip quivered. "Oh... I..."

"It wasn't only Mx. Hazelyn's relationship with Porntip that your grandmother disapproved of," Romy went on. "She had also found out some time ago that you and Yeshua, of all people, had become an item. A mere servant in her household. Your Po Po was bitterly disappointed. With your beauty, she had set her sights on one of the Yeoh or Tan grandsons for you. She had already decided to change her will and exclude you from it, even before she chanced upon Mx. Hazelyn and Porntip... in flagrante delicto."

Mamma mia, suddenly Romy could speak Italian.

"But how do you explain the door being locked from inside?" asked Dickson. "And we know Judith was in her room because when Bilal went to wake her, she was having a shower."

"Mr. Dickson, your Po Po's bathroom and Miss Judith's bathroom are side by side," Romy reminded him gently. "It was also several minutes before Bilal heard what he mistakenly thought was Miss Judith having a shower. The water running was actually from Po Po's bathroom. Miss Judith had to be absolutely certain that we had all left your grandmother's room before she could venture out of her hiding place and pretend to be in her own bathroom. It was an oversight on her part that she left behind the empty Amaretto bottle."

Judith's face went brick red. She was struggling between admission and denial. The desire to gloat couldn't be quelled. Admission won.

"Yes! Yes, I murdered Po Po. She had it coming. Yeshua and I, we love each other and we plan to marry and move to Sabah as soon as interstate travel is allowed, and install piped water for all the houses in his kampung. I'd broached the subject with Po Po. Asked her if I could maybe have an advance on my inheritance. But the old witch was furious! She just yelled at me, 'What for you want to help poor people you don't even know, haa? Haa?' Bejesus, I tell you, she sounded senile! Anyway, I thought I'd see first, if she would come round. But after a week, it was obvious she wasn't going to. That's when I decided enough was enough. Especially as there's talk of the government allowing more sectors to operate normally soon, which would include law firms. So last night, I waited till the old bag had settled in bed and Porntip was safely in her own room. Or Hazelyn's room," she added slyly. "Then I crept in to see Po Po, weeping and wailing, declaring I'd seen the light and begging for her forgiveness. In the end, she forgave me and I said, 'Po Po, I brought up a bottle of your favorite Amaretto from the liquor cabinet.'"

She was so pleased.

"That was when she uttered, 'Good girl, Judith, I'll drink to the newly reborn you!' And I watched her glug down that miniature bottle of Amaretto laced with fresh keluak which I'd blended into a fine paste. Then I laughed as I watched the old hag die."

There had been a brief moment of horrified silence after Judith poured out her confession.

Then, as if on cue, the doorbell had rung. It could only be the police.

Romy had heaved a sigh of relief. Time for him to go home and enjoy the rest of his birthday.

Just then, there had been a sudden movement. Followed by the sound of glass shattering onto the white Carrara marble floor.

"The Amaretto bottle!" Ashyon had exclaimed guiltily. "My fault, PI Romy. I didn't realize it was so near the edge of the table."

Romy had looked keenly at the four siblings. They met his eyes with a dispassionate, impenetrable gaze.

And he realized that, despite their dissensions and discord, when the crunch came and one of them was pushed to the wall, they understood the importance of family unity and the need to close ranks. Because blood was thicker than water. Their Ah Kong had taught them well.

"In the end, all we have is each other," Judith had said.

Which meant having each other's backs, always. And that was surely not a bad, but a good thing.

At the same time, he was suddenly reminded of an extract from a Taoist parable, which he had had to copy over and over again in his Hanzi class at primary school.

'Who knows what is good and what is bad?'

Ya, who knows? Romy ruminated, as he opened his Grab app to order a coffee. He still didn't feel *puas*, despite his hearty meal.

Great, there were lots of promos on Grab. Perhaps he would try this new place, which had opened not so long ago at Avenue K.

Their pecan praline latte sounded good. *To hell with the calories!* C'mon, guys, it was his birthday.

Sip sip, hooray!

The title of the above story was inspired by an almost similar title of a poem, 'The Road Not Taken', by the American poet Robert Frost (1874-1963).

Frost wrote the poem as a joke for his friend, Edward Thomas, also a poet, who was often unable to decide which route to take, when the two went on their walks during the three years, 1912 - 1915, Frost spent in England.

One day, as they were walking, they came across two roads. Thomas was indecisive and, in retrospect, often lamented that they should have taken the other one.

After Frost returned to America in 1915, he sent Thomas an advance copy of 'The Road Not Taken'. Thomas took the poem seriously and personally, and it may have been significant in his decision to enlist in the First World War.

Sadly, two years later in 1917, Thomas was killed in action at the Battle of Arras in France.

THE ROAD NOT TAKEN
by Robert Frost

Two roads diverged in a yellow wood,
And sorry I could not travel both
And be one traveler, long I stood
And looked down one as far as I could
To where it bent in the undergrowth;

Then took the other, as just as fair,
And having perhaps the better claim,
Because it was grassy and wanted wear;
Though as for that the passing there
Had worn them really about the same,

And both that morning equally lay
In leaves no step had trodden black.
Oh, I kept the first for another day!
Yet knowing how way leads on to way,
I doubted if I should ever come back.

I shall be telling this with a sigh
Somewhere ages and ages hence:
Two roads diverged in a wood, and I —
I took the one less traveled by,
And that has made all the difference.